Praise from Both Sides of the Atlantic for Ann C. Fallon's Mysteries

WHERE DEATH LIES

"As provocative as any murder you'll find in Agatha Christie or P. D. James."

—*Irish Voice*

"A delightful read. . . . Fallon's writing is lively and believable, her characters palpably real, and her impish sense of fun is allowed to emerge even in otherwise dramatic scenes."

—*Toronto Sunday Sun*

DEAD ENDS

"Ann C. Fallon's Ireland comes alive in haunting and sometimes gritty reality. Brilliant writing and a joy to read!"

—*Audrey Peterson*

"A first-rate murder mystery full of twists and turns. . . . Fallon really knows how to build up suspense and she k⬛⬛⬛⬛⬛⬛⬛⬛⬛⬛⬛⬛ begin-ning to end."

⬛⬛ *Echo*

"Complex. . . . R⬛⬛⬛⬛⬛⬛⬛⬛⬛⬛⬛⬛⬛⬛orth exploring for all armchair travelers and detectives."

—*Murder ad lib*

"A well-written and enjoyable mystery. . . . James Fleming is a fine Irish friend on a cold winter's night."

—*Murder & Mayhem*

Books by Ann C. Fallon

Blood Is Thicker
Dead Ends
Deadly Analysis
Potter's Field
Where Death Lies
Hour of Our Death

Published by POCKET BOOKS

For orders other than by individual consumers, Pocket Books grants a discount on the purchase of **10 or more** copies of single titles for special markets or premium use. For further details, please write to the Vice President of Special Markets, Pocket Books, 1230 Avenue of the Americas, 9th Floor, New York, NY 10020-1586.

For information on how individual consumers can place orders, please write to Mail Order Department, Simon & Schuster Inc., 100 Front Street, Riverside, NJ 08075.

Deadly Analysis

Ann C. Fallon

POCKET BOOKS
New York London Toronto Sydney Singapore

Quincy author

An *Original* Publication of POCKET BOOKS

 POCKET BOOKS, a division of Simon & Schuster Inc.
1230 Avenue of the Americas, New York, NY 10020

ISBN: 0-671-88516-2

First Pocket Books printing February 2000

10 9 8 7 6 5 4 3 2 1

POCKET and colophon are registered trademarks of
Simon & Schuster Inc.

Cover art by Griesbach/Martucci

Printed in the U.S.A.

To my dear friends,
the Murrays

CHAPTER

1

Dʀ. Thomas Darcy, psychiatrist and psychotherapist, closed the door behind his last patient that afternoon. Turning, he smiled tiredly at Mrs. Fogarty, who was finishing up a document on the computer.

"Long day?" she said sympathetically as she placed the papers together.

"Indeed," he said. "For you, too, I think."

Mrs. Fogarty beamed sweetly. She was a petite, dark-haired married woman in her thirties who lived nearby and came in a few hours each day, five days a week. Tom considered himself lucky. She was efficient, pleasant, warm, and discreet. Her children were young and at school, and her husband, he suspected, was a heavy drinker. Tom knew that she enjoyed her job, and admired her kindness with his patients. She was also competent at the bookkeeping, and he dreaded the day she would leave him for a more demanding job. Not that she had ever indicated any intention to leave. She handed him the case notes that she had typed and removed her coat from the hook on the back of the door.

"Till tomorrow then," he said.

"Good night, Dr. Darcy," she said, smiling. "You'll lock up the files?"

"As always."

"Right, then, I'm off."

Darcy returned to his office. Pensive, preoccupied with the troubling session he'd just had, he sat at his desk, quickly making salient notes about his patient, Mary, and the problems she had recounted to him. His thick graying hair fell forward onto his brow as he bent in concentration. Of medium build, he had shoulders that were slightly bowed, and his face showed the gentle frown lines of a man habitually concerned and attentive. His was an intense expression, his blue eyes behind the half glasses revealed a deep intelligence and told of a rich but not always happy life.

Tom finished his written notes, placing them methodically in a marked manila folder. He stood and unlocked the low filing cabinet that ran the length of the narrower end of the rectangular room. Filing the folder away, as well as the typed notes which Mrs. Fogarty had given him, he closed the heavy drawer and relocked it, placing the key on his desk. Checking the pages of his desk diary to refresh his memory as to his schedule for the following day, he sighed and closed the book and slipped it into the drawer of his wide mahogany desk.

Tom turned to the small closet along the left wall of his spacious office. It felt good to shed the dark blue chalk-striped wool suit he'd opted for as his formal dress when he began his practice, and to change into a pair of well-worn corduroy trousers and a heavy heather gray flecked pullover. He checked his attaché case, ascertaining that his Filofax was safely stowed there. Removing the handheld tape recorder, he transferred it to the deep pockets of his trousers along with the cabinet key. Picking up his suit and surveying the desk and filing cabinet again in a somewhat obsessive-compulsive way, as he noted wryly to himself, he finally left his office, locking it behind him.

On his way now, he checked his outer office, a comfortable waiting room with low table lamps, soft lighting, a radio paying classical music, and magazines that were always up to date but which remained unread by his distracted patients. Mrs. Fogarty's desk was bare, the phone still, the computer covered; all was in good order. He turned off the lights and the radio and locked this door, too, behind him.

His sense of isolation, of which he was barely aware, was intensified as he stepped into the softly carpeted corridor, passing the doors of the building's other occupants. He could hear the sounds of phones ringing, of chatting, of other, fellow human beings getting on with things. He left them behind, aware that they neither knew nor cared whether or when he came and went.

Dr. Darcy's office was one of four en suite in a modern purpose-built building on the outskirts

of Dublin, near the village of Dundrum. Clean,
spare, characterless, he found the building itself
wasn't to his personal taste, but the location was
convenient for his practice: easily accessible for
his patients, with a small car park next to it and
a bus stop close by.

Tom Darcy eased his dark blue BMW out of
the crowded car park and into the pleasure of a
soft Irish early evening in mid-autumn. Soft in
that the rain was a version of mist, and when the
sun did choose to shine, as it did now, there was
still warmth in its rays. Tom could feel its healing
power on his arm as he leaned it on the open
window of his car.

He drove without haste to the south, toward
Enniskerry and the riding stables there. He had
taken out his tape recorder with the idea that he'd
make a few more notes regarding Mary, but as he
drove, he let the problems and woes of the day and
its patients drift out of his mind and allowed the
view of the fields and their autumnal browns and
reds and golds fill his eyes and soothe his spirit.

The wheels of the car crunched on the gravel
as he pulled into the yard abutting the stable
area. The sound triggered off a memory, and he
was caught up again with worry about Mary and
how she had found herself driving at some distance from her house, not knowing how she got
there. He shook his head. "That's not what I am
here for now," he muttered to himself, as he
habitually did when he knew himself to be alone.
No. Riding was to clear his head of every conscious thought and unconscious association.

He felt his mood lift as he anticipated the energetic gallop through the fields. Walking briskly toward the stable yard, he only then noticed the unusual number of people clustering at the entrance to the main stable, which housed the privately owned horses.

As if suddenly thrown into a dream, he watched all, or it seemed all, of the people turn their heads with one accord and stare at him. Knowing they couldn't be looking for him, he turned and looked over his shoulder, expecting to see someone else following behind him.

There was no one.

He walked on.

"Dr. Darcy!" The owner of the stables, a well-built, strappingly healthy woman in her fifties, advanced toward him with long powerful strides.

"Dr. Darcy," she repeated and held out her hand.

Surprised, he shook it. "Mrs. Killian?" She held his hand between her own.

"Come," she said, drawing him toward her own house at some remove from the stable and the crowd.

Alarm now filled him. His mind raced, sorting through myriad possibilities and rejecting them all. This was, after all, neutral territory—neither hospital nor office nor home—and he relaxed slightly.

"I'm afraid I have some very shocking and disturbing news," Mrs. Killian said in her brusque manner, which had always reminded Tom of fictional colonels in fictional British armies in a fictional India.

"Yes," he replied slowly, caught by the word "shocking"—no, this surely did not involve him, "shocking" had connotations that would not apply to him or his work. He consciously distanced himself from any possibility of real involvement in whatever had happened.

"Your horse, your beloved horse." Her voice thickened.

"Quixote?" he exclaimed.

"Yes, Quixote. I'm terribly sorry, but she's dead."

Years of training allowed him to not cry out. The cry came up his gorge and into his mouth. It was stopped there by the clenching of his teeth. Anger seeped into his face.

"Was there an accident?" he said severely, pulling his hand away from her unwelcome comforting clasp. "Was someone riding her? Have you put her down?"

Darcy turned unconsciously toward the stable and then back.

"What do mean she's dead?" he said abruptly, reality sinking in.

"Brendan, you know Brendan, the stable boy. He went into the stalls to get Quixote warmed up and saddled in time for your arrival. When he saw the stall empty he thought the horse was in the ring, although this surprised him. But, you see," Mrs. Killian paused, drawing breath, "the stall wasn't empty. Quixote was there, but when Brendan didn't see her head looking out from the half door, he went to the ring and then to the yard. When he didn't find her he assumed one of the lads had taken Quixote up the field to graze.

Brendan decided he might as well take advantage of the opportunity, so to speak, to muck out Quixote's stall. That was when he opened the door and . . . dear God . . . wasn't Quixote there all the time . . . lying dead."

Tom turned again toward the stable. "Heart attack?" he said with resignation.

"Well, we've contacted the large animal vet in Wicklow. I think he'll tell us . . ."

She seemed to him less than forthcoming.

"Tell us what?"

She didn't answer.

"I'd like to see her," Darcy said forcefully.

"Yes, I knew that you would." She took a step. "Listen, Dr. Darcy, it wasn't a heart attack."

"Then you do know what it was. For Chrissakes, just tell me." Darcy began to move off, annoyed with her lack of frankness.

"No, wait. Dr. Darcy. I do believe that Quixote was . . ."

"Yes, yes?"

"She was murdered."

CHAPTER

2

Tom stood at the door of the stable staring almost without comprehension at the body of his beloved mare.

Blood was everywhere despite the mounds of straw the stable lads had piled around the lifeless body to stem the flow escaping into the gutter that ran the length of the stalls. Great black globs of blood stood coagulating in pools of brighter crimson. The horse was on its side, her beautiful neck curved in an unnatural angle, the head still graceful, still striking in death, as was the long forehead, and the proud lift of the nostrils. Tom couldn't see the wound. He assumed it was in the chest, the heart, perhaps the neck. Clinically he registered that an artery had been severed, which would account for so much, so very much blood. The people around him stood awed at the sight of the horse, stunned into a dreadful speechlessness at the sight of Dr. Darcy finally kneeling in the straw and stroking the white splash of color on the forehead of his animal, that one spot of white still untouched by blood. The smell was overpowering. Blood and straw. Blood and muck. Blood and caking red mud.

Darcy stood, oblivious of the blood on his knees.

"Well . . ." he said, turning toward Mrs. Killian, his eyes burning in his gray face. "Who did this?" His voice was softer than they expected, and it sent shivers through the listeners. He glared balefully at them, not taking in faces or details, but viewing them suddenly as mortal enemies. He recovered himself, stiffening his back in an habitual gesture.

"Please, Dr. Darcy, please come with me." Mrs. Killian opened her hand in a beckoning gesture and they walked slowly toward the house.

"I'm so sorry, Doctor. I, too, loved Quixote, you must know that . . ."

Darcy was silent. He was so familiar with the egotism, the narcissism, of his patients. He recognized it now in Mrs. Killian. Yes, you're sad, but so am I, he interpreted her as saying. But he was having none of it. This was his loss, his grief, his anger.

"I asked you once already: who did this?" They stood in the gathering gloam waiting for the vet to arrive.

"I can tell you nothing," she said simply. "There were four other horses in their stalls at the same time. Why would anyone kill a horse?" She turned to look back at the animals in the paddock. "And why was Quixote killed and not

another? I have no answers. But I can tell you
how sorry I am . . ."

Tom felt his limbs starting to tremble, and
some of the anger dwindled away. "I'll need to
ring the police, I imagine," he said, sighing with
fatigue.

"Of course. I can make the call if you like."

"Is there anyone working here, do you think,
who could have . . . ?" Darcy looked into the middle distance.

"Someone in my stables who would be capable
of such a thing? God no!" Mrs. Killian exclaimed.
"I know that in my heart and soul." Her voice
rose. "I know these lads and girls, and that's all
they are, Doctor, that's all they are. Children
besotted with horses. They love them better than
their families . . . and rightly so," she added.

"I can't . . . can't take it in. Evil," he muttered.
"Evil, evil, pure evil."

Mrs. Killian shifted her stance uneasily at this.
And it was with a certain relief that she spotted the
vet's car approaching down the curve of the drive.

A young man, short and muscular, sprang
from the battered, mud-spattered car. Leaving
the door open in his haste, he ran toward them
with his black bag.

"I just got the message and they said it was
urgent, very urgent. What, what is it?" He
stopped, looking at their grim faces.

"It's a horse . . ."

"I assume so!" he said gruffly. "Which horse?"

"It's Quixote, you might remember her, the one
with the auburn mane?"

"Yes, yes, well, is it her leg or what?" He moved quickly toward the stable yard.

"The horse is dead," Mrs. Killian said flatly. "We don't know how, but there's a great deal of blood," she called after him as the vet ran toward the stall.

CHAPTER

—— 3 ——

JAMES FLEMING, HIS curly black hair tousled, which was indicative of his agitation, pulled his deep green Citroën into the last remaining parking space on level two of the car park at the Dublin airport. In silence he leapt from the car, and with his long loping stride he reached an empty luggage cart and returned in time to open the passenger door.

"Thanks," Sarah said tersely as she stepped out.

"Mm," murmured James, preoccupied with extracting the massive number of her Louis Vuitton bags from the boot.

James's deep brown eyes and handsome face, even paler now than was usual, were troubled as he piled the bags efficiently on a luggage trolley and clicked his remote. The two passenger doors locked with a satisfying *thunnk*.

"What time is your flight again?" he asked

rhetorically, sensing that this parting might be more fraught than most.

Some hours later as James approached the solitary figure standing at the outer gates of St. James Hospital, he saw, or imagined he saw, Geraldine's stony expression.

He didn't imagine it. As he began to hurry toward her, his suit jacket flapping in the wind, he saw that she was becoming even more Medusa-like, and as he grew closer, he could see her shoulder-length black hair whipping around her face like the mythical snakes.

"I'm sorry," he shouted even before reaching her side.

"I'll have your guts for garters!" she exploded. "Do you know what I feel like, waiting here like a schoolgirl being stood up on a date?"

"The traffic."

"Oh really?"

"Well, the departing flight was slightly delayed, fog in London . . ."

"And you had to hold her hand, didn't you? The famous Miss Sarah Heartburn couldn't wait in the super VIP lounge by herself?" Geraldine's voice went up on the last word.

"Come, let's walk on to the pub. The traffic here is ridiculous, and I'm parked way down at the corner."

Geraldine strode on ahead of him. James saw the stubborn set of her naturally square shoulders cloaked in the fine olive green gabardine trench coat. As the breeze abated, her black hair, shiny as always, fell back into place. He didn't even try to catch up to her, although three long steps would have accomplished that. He walked behind her, watching her march in her high black heels, her black leather tote bag swinging from her shoulder. They walked this way in royal fashion until she finally reached the door of Ryan's pub.

She stood waiting, her face softened now by the exercise and the reemergence of her easygoing nature.

"I'm still angry," she said, but she neither looked nor sounded it.

"Come on, I'll explain inside," James said softly, taking her elbow as he opened the heavy oak and glass door.

They were in luck. Their favorite snug at the front end of the long bar was vacant. They squeezed onto the narrow, dark-vinyl-clad bench and closed the door. Geraldine tapped on the small rectangle of glass, which opened eventually. A hand was seen on the scarred bar, and a voice came from somewhere behind.

"What'll it be?"

The voice was never inviting, but patrons found this part of the charm.

"Two pints of Guinness," James said with authority. The door shut.

This process of ordering always left James in a state of doubt. Had he been heard? Should he knock again? When, if ever, would the drinks appear? It was all taken on trust.

"So are you driving home, or what?" said Geraldine as they waited.

"Aaah . . ." James hesitated. "Well, as you know, I brought the car . . ."

"And?"

"All right, just one drink for me." James was annoyed, being chided like a teenager.

"Well, I'm walking, and I intend to let my hair down, metaphorically speaking." She grinned, teasing him. "Now, tell me, why were you so late?"

"I do apologize." James loosened his tie and undid the buttons on his waistcoat. She smiled, since he only did this when he began to relax.

"I know all that," she said sweetly.

"The flight really was delayed. Unfortunately." He grimaced. "Sarah didn't want to wait alone. And so we did wait together in the VIP lounge. She had a mineral water and then she . . ." He hesitated. "Well, it was at that auspicious moment she decided to deliver her . . ."

"Ultimatum?"

"Yes."

Suddenly the little rectangular door opened and two pints of Guinness were banged down on the narrow ledge. Blobs of brownish creamy foam flew in all directions. James placed a ten-pound note on the wood, where it quickly absorbed the foam. A veined hand took the money and banged the door shut. James was grateful for the interruption and he drank slowly, not caring that the liquid ran down the glass and onto his knees. It was a brown suit anyway, he consoled himself.

Geraldine, too, sipped slowly, and then extracted one of her pungent Gauloises cigarettes from her pocket. She inhaled lightly and blue smoke floated around their heads.

"And what was this ultimatum?" Her voice held the slightest edge.

James studied the drops on the knees of his suit. He sighed at last. "Very simple really. It's either Sarah or you." Avoiding Geraldine's eyes, he took another sip, deeper this time.

"I see . . . well, it seems to me that that makes a great deal of sense."

"Oh, Ger, you've been so patient. Please . . ." James's voice was gentle, and unintentionally he influenced her feelings.

"Too patient, if anyone bothered to ask me." She kept up her formidable exterior, blowing smoke into his face.

"Here, let me have one of those," he said.

She pushed the pack toward him. A heavy silence followed.

"Listen, Ger," James said finally. "I've known Sarah longer than I've known you . . ."

She started to object, but bit her tongue.

"And I came to know her under very strange circumstances. There's a bond there, between us, that tugs at us any time I begin to pull away . . ."

"Or when she begins to pull away," Geraldine added, her tone sharp.

"All right, I admit that's true too."

His face grew sad as he studied the tip of his cigarette.

Geraldine put out her hand hesitantly and touched his. Her long crimson nails lightly grazed his skin. He shivered.

"I don't think it's love . . ." she whispered.

"Nor do I, but apparently it's just as strong," he said.

"What is as strong as love?" she murmured, her voice rich and full.

Again silence.

"Hate?" James looked startled even as he said it. Geraldine jumped inadvertently and pulled away her hand. "I don't believe that," she said.

"No, no, nor do I," said James hastily. "It just fell out of my mouth." He rubbed his eyes wearily. "I had a long day at work. Walter had some trouble—it's a conveyance but very messy, the check bounced. Oh, it's boring for you but a bit troublesome for us."

"Right, then," Ger said brightly, changing the subject. "Listen, there's a dance at the hospital on Halloween weekend."

"A staff dance?" James asked with interest.

"No. A dance for the medium-term patients. The staff decorate the hall and stand around the walls, we serve up a nice nonalcoholic punch while the patients mingle and sometimes even dance."

"Oh, the mind boggles," James said, smiling. He imagined the mentally disturbed patients she dealt with in her capacity as resident at the hospital dancing around in this strange setting and he immediately tapped on the window to attempt to order another round. The two of them then settled in for a cozy evening, silently but mutually agreeing, yet again, to set aside James's dilemma.

CHAPTER
—— 4 ——

TOM DARCY SAGGED onto the seat of his car. The previous hour seemed a blur to him. Killian's horrifying news, the vet's arrival, the visit of the local police, Killian's arrangements for a necropsy at her own expense, the unanswered questions.

He leaned forward, put the key in the ignition, and paused. The police said they would come by his office. What a mistake. What was he thinking when he agreed to that? His patients would flee. Or some of them anyway. He would have to prevent that.

He would need a lawyer, he thought resignedly. And he thought of Joan, his wife. Even if he called her, would she care? The horse had meant nothing to her. Or perhaps that had been a pretense; perhaps she'd seen her as a rival. He sighed. He could not bear, at this moment, to deal with someone who was not empathic to his sorrow.

Leaving the key unturned in the ignition, Tom resorted to his never before used cellular phone. His concession had been to get one for emergencies. Little did he think then that this would be the occasion. His mind was blank. He was so weary he felt he couldn't drag himself out of the car, unlock the boot, unlock the briefcase, to get his address book.

Staring blankly out the windscreen, he tried to remember the name, any name, of a lawyer, even of someone who knew a lawyer. What had he to do with lawyers? Unwillingly he saw again in his mind's eye the body of his beloved horse. He began to turn his head, to look back over his shoulder toward the stables, but the muscles of his neck rebelled, warning him not to do this.

He stared instead at the trees in front of him, darkening, darkening into night.

He stared at the phone, dead in his hand.

He forced his memory to function. There was the solicitor who'd helped them over the new house. New! He nearly laughed. What was it? Eight years ago now. But he still thought of it as the new house. Concentrate. Focus, he reprimanded himself. What was the man's name?

It was an ordinary name. Protestant-sounding. How did he find him back then? They knew someone mutually. Yes, another MD. But who? He mentally scrolled through names, hitting upon that of James. A tall fellow. A bit diffident. Like his brother. It was the brother he knew. Their last name? He felt the dark that was not night creeping in on him. No, he must avoid that.

F. It was an F. A surname. Wait, it was coming. He closed his eyes. Fallon? No, no. More Protestant than that. Yes. A Protestant name. Flemish? No, nearly there. Fleming!

Quickly he dialed Directory Inquiries. Asking for the listing of Dr. Fleming, he quickly dialed again, only to receive an answering service. Yes. Yes. An emergency. The girl on the other end was frightened as he nearly shouted into the phone. Oh, yes, he too was a physician. He must speak to Dr. Fleming.

Finally, Donald Fleming's voice on the line, curious, but careful. Yes, he had a brother in the law. The number, yes of course, the unfinished thank-yous.

Yet another answering service. He left the message and disconnected, despondent. The darkness was now complete.

Knowing better, but knowing also he couldn't phone home for a lift, he engaged the engine and pulled slowly out onto the narrow road. He drove in first gear, down the steep, winding road, distracted and preoccupied. Slowly he pulled onto the main road. Time passed. Why? How? The sound of an incessantly beeping horn finally impinged on his consciousness. He glanced in his mirror, seeing a line of double lights following him along the narrow road through the gorge outside Enniskerry known as the Scalp. No one able to pass. He shook himself. He was leading a funeral procession, he thought. He regained his composure and shifted, speeding up, wanting only to be home, to be out of this car, to be off the road. Still the cars, still the long line of head-lights. A desperate driver overtook the car behind him and then his own.

Where to pull over? He saw the row of cottages on his left, charming and neat as always, so inviting now with lights shining in their windows, so welcoming in the darkness. He remembered that up ahead was a pub. A large car park. It had a literary name. Yes, the Golden Bowl.

Approaching the pub, he put on his left indicator light, slowed, and stopped, halting the funeral procession entirely. He waited until the lorry oncoming had passed safely and then he pulled across into the car park. He thought he could hear the bitter cheers of the twenty drivers who picked up speed and flew on into the night.

He turned off the engine and rested his head on the steering wheel. A brandy, he thought.

Once inside he rang through to Joan; she'd get a friend and they'd collect him and the car. Her voice was distant. He didn't care.

Yes, he did. As he sipped the double brandy he noticed his hands were trembling. God, what a day!

CHAPTER

—— 5 ——

THE NEXT MORNING James groaned as he rose from his bachelor bed. What a pain in the arse! Metaphorically speaking. The Citröen was halfway across town. He'd have to take a taxi over and then drive back to the office in morning traffic. First things first, however.

James's service had phoned him around midnight; he was to return an urgent call. Which he had. Not quite sober, he had made the call and reached the doctor's own answering machine.

Annoyed at the time by this kind of telephone tag, James had left a terse message. No better one than a doctor for such things. Must be some friend of Donald, he thought.

James was still thinking of Donald as he dressed for the day. He had deliberately avoided seeing his brother since he started going out with Geraldine. His brother had dated Geraldine, after a fashion, and James was forced to admit to the face in the mirror that he was apprehensive that Donald was still interested, and might perhaps act on that interest, or even try to date her again out of some perverse competitive spirit. Geraldine, Geraldine. It was clear from her manner of the night before that she wasn't going to stand for being "the other woman." James swore as he sliced his chin with a new blade and drew blood.

Calming down, he also admitted to himself that Ger in fact was the other woman. A mental picture of Sarah obscured his vision. She would be on New York time now. No doubt, having already risen from her solitary cool bed, having jogged with her friends around Central Park, she was now doing lunch at Le Cirque. Slim, self-possessed, Sarah. As unreachable there as she was when she was beside him.

Not in good form at all, he dialed for a taxi and clomped down the stairs to the pavement, only to return for his briefcase and start all over again.

Tom Darcy also rose early from his bed, still groggy from the exhaustion and the brandy of the night before. His wife was up before him, as usual. He sat for a while on the edge of the rumpled bed, steadying himself physically and mentally, allowing the reality of the events of the day before to seep in gently from the circumference of his mind. Rubbing his face with both hands, he finally stood up and began his morning toilet.

When he reached the gleaming fashionable Poggenphol kitchen on the ground floor of his substantial detached house, the coffee was ready.

Joan, his wife of nearly twenty-five years, was already standing by the back door. She was, as usual, impeccably dressed, today in a well-cut, cream-colored suit. Her hair, reddened to a youthful chestnut, a color he noted idly to himself that was nothing like her own, was gleaming.

Briskly she checked her handbag, withdrawing her keys. "I'm off now, Tom," she said without catching his eye.

"Right, then," he said wearily.

"Coffee's there."

"So I see." Tom's tone was neutral. He knew Joan wanted always to find a hint of sarcasm in his succinct, neutral statements. But it was never there.

She turned toward the kitchen door, which led to the narrow cement path, nearly lost in the abundance of this autumn's mums and hardy geraniums. It would lead her to the two cars, one behind the other in the driveway. Her own dark red "Beemer," with the custom interior, was waiting. But she hesitated.

"Cheerio," she said at last to his continued silence. "Don't forget to contact the police, they rang earlier. Number's by the phone."

"Thank you," Tom said. "I never heard the phone ringing."

He watched her leave the room, her once slim but big-boned frame now stout and solid yet still energetic. If he saw her from the back, in a queue perhaps, he mused, he never would have known her to be that young woman with the long flowing hair that blew in the wind on the top of Three

Rock Mountain that day he knew he'd fallen in love.

The unexpected shrill ring of the timer bell on the microwave broke his reverie. She'd left him his breakfast. Efficient as ever. Yet not one word had she spoken about Quixote or his loss. When she'd met him at the pub she'd been quick and businesslike, introducing him to her friend and getting his keys from him. Her friend had driven his car; he'd ridden in silence with Joan in hers. Yet it was a silence imposed by Joan. Oppressed by the memory, he successfully blocked it out. It had become a habit now, not wanting to examine his own wife's behavior toward him.

He withdrew the warmed-over sausages and rashers from the oven and, revolted at the sight, placed them on the floor for the cat. Resolved now to face the business of the day, he went to the phone to place yet another call to Fleming. Meeting with no success there, he phoned the police and reluctantly arranged the time he would come in to the station to discuss Quixote. With a heavy heart and a heavy step on the stairs he went to his empty room to dress and prepare to leave his silent house.

Around the time that Tom Darcy had been grimly reflecting on his wife's coldness, James had arrived at his office on Merrion Square. His mood was high again, altered by a spectacularly bright Dublin autumn day, and he bounded up the stairs to his first-floor office. Maggie, his volatile, red-haired office manager, was there before him.

"You just had a call, James," she said without any other greeting. Her tone stopped him in mid-stride, halfway from the door to her desk.

"No hello, no good morning?" he said, failing to hide his hurt. He thought he was used to her tones, but this was harsh even by Maggie's standards.

"If you came in on time there'd be room for such pleasantries, James." She looked pointedly at the clock, which was reading a comfortable 9:45 as its burnished pendulum swung back and forth, catching the morning light from the high Georgian windows.

"Maggie, Dublin doesn't start functioning until ten and you know it. The *Times* must be read and digested along with the coffee."

"Yes, well, the medical community doesn't adhere to your old bankers' hours, James. Dr. Darcy rang at the stroke of nine, fully expecting you to be at your desk."

"Darcy, is it? Well, I rang him last night and—" He stopped himself. Surely this was beneath him, to defend himself to Maggie. She never failed to get him riled. After all, who was in charge here?

But he couldn't help himself. "Donald keeps more limited hours than I do . . ."

"Whatever your problems with the debonair Donald, leave them at home, James. This is Doctor Darcy . . ." She looked at him expectantly.

"One of Donald's friends, no doubt."

"You did the conveyance on his house."

"Yes, but . . ."

"James, he's a highly respected psychiatrist . . ."
James still looked blank.

"Right, right." But Maggie's derisive tone had made James uneasy. Ever the conscientious solicitor, he had Maggie get Darcy on the line.

After listening to Darcy's succinct explanation of events, James, his curiosity piqued, agreed to meet him at the police station in Stepaside.

The rush hour traffic had abated and James enjoyed his route out of town and into the nearby countryside. The sky was a pale but brilliant blue and fallen leaves flew before him twirling in mini-tornadoes, reminding him of the stories of the *sidhe* he'd heard in school.

The tiny hamlet was quiet. A few locals were gathered at the bookies. The pub-cum-restaurant nearby was just coming awake after its late night.

James saw a well-dressed professional man he assumed to be Darcy standing near a dark BMW. His graying black hair was disheveled by the morning breeze; his face seemed faintly familiar but the expression was worn. As they shook hands James noted that the strength and warmth of the grip belied the tired blue eyes that scrutinized him.

"Fleming? I'm Tom, Tom Darcy," he said in a soft voice. "Thanks for coming. As I said on the phone, I don't need a solicitor, but I wanted someone . . . you . . . in on this from the start." He looked into James's eyes as if to read something there. James was strangely moved.

"Certainly," he said brusquely. "I'll do what I can."

Together they entered the narrow corridor that

led into the police station and they approached a high wooden desk. All was painted cream and green and gleamed in the bright morning light.

A young policeman greeted Darcy by name and led them to a scarred wooden table. They refused his offer of instant coffee and he efficiently set about taking down the details.

As Darcy reiterated the events of the day before, James was struck by his demeanor. He hadn't seen a man so defeated in quite a while. He began now to recall his first impressions of years ago, and somehow the two sets of observations did not jibe. The fact the man was eight years older might contribute to it, but the Darcy he remembered was vital, energetic, and decisive. These attributes seemed missing today. James shifted his attention to Darcy's words.

"We have the details from the man who visited the scene," the young garda repeated. "Please, just tell me why you think this happened."

Darcy's voice deepened with emotion.

"I have no insight," he said resignedly, "into why someone could or would kill an animal of that grace and beauty and gentleness. However, let me see . . ." He cleared his throat. "I purchased her about four years ago, and from the beginning I stabled her at Mrs. Killian's. I think she is known to you?"

The policeman nodded.

"It was a convenient location for me. Not far from my home or office. I had ridden at her stables for years, and when I bought Quixote, she helped me. In fact she recommended that I buy the horse. The owners were moving abroad. They sold her willingly and I bought willingly."

"Ah," said the young man. "Well, then. Maybe the person who killed the horse was out for revenge—revenge against the original owner?" he said hopefully.

James leaned forward. Perhaps this young garda had found a neat solution.

But Darcy snapped at him. "How can that be? Firstly, the horse came from County Kildare, secondly, I've owned her for over four years. And to top it off, I changed her name and it's been registered."

"I agree that's all true, Darcy," James interjected, "but you know, horse people can easily trace a horse if they are determined."

"Then why now—after four years?" Darcy sank back in his chair.

"Perhaps the killer was also out of the country, perhaps the killer was incarcerated and recently released." The young garda held his ground.

This gave Darcy pause. He sighed softly.

"I like your theory." He smiled for the first time. "At least it gives me a little relief to think that Quixote's killing wasn't aimless, inexplicable vandalism." James had the strong sense that Darcy was grasping at straws, but nonetheless joined in.

"Let's talk about the original owner," said James, and the policeman nodded.

Darcy reflected for a moment. "I've had no contact with them since I bought the horse. I have the bill of sale and other papers in my files. The name was O'Connell." He paused. "This doesn't make sense. You see, he was a large-animal vet. A wife. Two children, young. It had been his own horse for three years."

"Why was he leaving Ireland?" The garda poised his pen.

"His wife was Canadian. She had family there. He was willing to try living there."

"Perhaps they came back? Have you had any contact with them since?"

"No, I said that. Look," Darcy was getting impatient. "We weren't friends. I'm surprised I remember this much detail. The horse went up for sale. I'd looked at a few others. Mrs. Killian came with me and had the expertise I lacked. The horse was healthy, a good age for my simple purposes. The papers were in order. I met the owner once when we went to view the horse, and once again when I bought her. Mrs. Killian was with me both times and she helped me with the horse box rental and all that."

"So he could be back?" pressed the young garda. "The original owner?" Darcy shifted irritably in his chair.

James intervened smoothly. "I think Dr. Darcy doesn't have any more information on that point. He needs to return to his patients. If there is anything else?"

"Yes." The garda glared at James and then turned back to Darcy.

"Do you have any enemies, Dr. Darcy? Someone who would want to get at you?"

James noticed Darcy shiver almost imperceptibly.

"Of course not," said Darcy in a modulated voice. "I really must be going." He stood up abruptly and, nodding almost imperiously to both men, left the room.

Partly to mollify the policeman and partly to satisfy his own questions, James hung back.

"You know, it needn't have been aimed at Dr. Darcy directly. This killing could have been aimed at Mrs. Killian, and the horse chosen at random," he said as he stood up.

"Yes, we've thought of that, Mr. Fleming. We're pursuing our inquiries in many directions."

James was surprised to see Darcy still standing in the car park. As he approached him, he took note of the dress and demeanor of the man. Now he had the time to note the contrast between Darcy's rather thrown-together appearance and the good quality of his clothing—the very fine chalk-striped suit with the waistcoat hastily buttoned; single-needle tailored pure white shirt with a good silk tie haphazardly knotted.

"I thought you had patients?" James asked.

"I do, but not until this afternoon. I just wanted to . . ." He paused, his eyes wandering to the clear blue sky above the police station.

"How about a coffee then?" said James cheerily, anxious to speak with the man about all that he did not know. They arranged to meet in a half hour's time in town.

Bewley's of Grafton Street was jammed as usual. They elbowed their way into the lag end of the queue and balanced their coffee and currant buns on shaky trays. James, the taller of the two, spotted an empty table in the farthest corner and headed for it aggressively. As they placed their cups on the small sticky table, James sighed aloud.

"What's the story?" asked Darcy, smiling.

"I was merely thinking of how nice it was, you know, when I was at Trinity. To come in and to be served. To have a cigarette with my coffee and eye the girls at the other tables, or stretch my legs at the fire. This was one of my favorite corners."

"Along with half of Dublin," Darcy returned. "Us UCD types came here too, before the whole college upped and moved."

"Oh, Dublin's changed . . . beyond recognition . . ." James looked so forlorn that Darcy actually laughed.

"Sorry, Fleming, but we do sound like two aul' wans, don't we?"

"Maybe you're right." James smiled and bit into his currant bun. "But you must admit that Dublin has changed in the last twenty years. Now I remember . . ."

"Please, please, good things are happening to the city too."

"Do I hear a professional tone there, Darcy?"

"Occupational hazard, I'm afraid."

"Hardly a hazard, is it?"

"It can be to oneself, I think." Darcy drifted off again. James was intrigued by the chameleon nature of Darcy's moods.

"You can't put a positive spin on this event, though . . ."

Darcy glanced up from his coffee, the currant bun untouched on his plate.

"I loved that horse, Fleming," he said passionately.

"I can empathize but . . ."

"I tell you," Darcy said, "that horse knew me. She was a partner. She knew my moods. Oh, I realize this sounds fanciful, but she did. After a difficult day, and if I could steal the time, I'd take her out. I'd ride for hours. Not hard, mind you. But I'd ride and somehow my mood would lift. There was a closeness between man and beast that I haven't . . ."

Darcy suddenly turned his head away, leaving his sentence unfinished. He looked back quickly and smiled again, a quick, ironic smile.

"You know, Darcy, I think it's entirely possible that this crime was not directed at you personally. My guess is it was aimed at the stable, in other words, the owner, Mrs. Killian, for some sick reason, but for a reason nonetheless."

"Go on," said Darcy rather solemnly.

Uneasily, James continued, feeling all of a sudden that he was being scrutinized.

"Well, as you know, I do mostly conveyancing, real estate, wills, and so on."

"Of course, you did that for me."

"And that's why you phoned me?"

Darcy nodded.

"Over the years, various other kinds of cases have come my way, not in a strictly legal sense. Problems, difficult situations. I have been of some assistance and I've had some success."

"Can you tell me about those?" Darcy said softly, his professional manner asserting itself unconsciously.

Again James was reticent, self-conscious.

"Well, obviously a lot of it was confidential."

"Of course. I of all people should appreciate that fact."

Darcy took his checkbook from the inside pocket of his suit jacket. Looking up, he said, "Fleming. It's James, right?"

"Yes."

"I would like you to look into this for me. I'd prefer to think that the death of Quixote was either a mindless violent act or, as you suggest, related somehow to the stables, or even . . ."

"Related in some way to the previous owner, as the police seem to think?"

"Yes. I want to give you a retainer, so that we have a distinctly professional relationship." Darcy raised an eyebrow and looked questioningly at James.

"By all means." James nodded. "And then anything we discuss will be protected by privilege?"

"You take my point, Fleming." Darcy scribbled out a check and handed it to James

It was for quite a substantial amount. He extended his hand to Darcy.

"James, please. Call me James."

They shook hands firmly, but Darcy's hand was as cold as ice.

CHAPTER

6

JAMES AND GERALDINE were walking the length of Dun Laoghaire pier, an old habit of James's but a new and unwelcome one for Geraldine.

"All right, James. We've done this twice, both ways. By my count that's four opportunities to see the same view and pass the same O.A.P.s and mothers with pushchairs."

"What! It's windswept and raining. There are only a dozen people out here."

"My point exactly. And now there'll be eleven." Geraldine turned on her heel and marched off toward the roadway and James's Citroën. Her pink chiffon scarf, sodden with rain mixed with the spray from the surf that was beginning to build and crash against the supporting wall, hung around her shoulders.

James stared after her, annoyed. He walked a few yards more, but then he too turned back. When he reached his car, he couldn't see into it.

He'd given Ger his spare key and never minded when she borrowed the car, usually to impress some friend from out of town. But this! This was intolerable.

He pulled open the driver's door and got in.

"Geraldine, for God's sake." He waved his hand dramatically. "Isn't it enough the car is steamed up, without adding smoke to it."

Ger stared straight ahead into the smoke.

"You at least could have started the engine and got some heat going!" James took the keys off her lap and inserted the ignition key. The engine responded and purred contentedly, soothing his nerves. He backed out of the space, pulled forward out of the car park, and edged up to the traffic light.

"Ger, what is the matter?" he asked more calmly.

"We don't seem to be on the same track, James. Not now, not ever."

"Oh God, not again."

"No, not 'Oh God,'" she snapped. "I think it's true. I think we should talk. And I also think that your 'oh Gods' are a way to stop us from talking."

"Right," he said, but he was exasperated. All he had wanted was a brisk walk to clear his head at the end of the day.

He said as much.

"That might be fine, James, if I'd had any warning or if I was dressed for it. Look at me."

She slowly unwrapped her limp scarf and shook her straight black hair. Her shoes appeared to him to be all right, but the splatters on her legs were large and muddy. She dabbed at them ineffectually with a bunched up, damp tissue.

"I see your point," he said as he sped into traffic back toward Dublin.

Silence fell. The walk had done him no good. Their date was doing him no good. But the silence couldn't continue like this either.

"Let's try that pub near you, the one with the fireplace, hmm?"

Geraldine didn't answer, but as she dried out from the heat of the car, she began to dust the mud off her skirt and to comb out her hair. She even applied her bright red lipstick.

Since it was relatively early they were able to obtain the two seats nearest the fire. James ordered Ger's usual G and T and a Guinness for himself. He ran his hands through his curly dark brown hair in a way she loved but had never told him. Her eyes softened.

"Shall we start again," she said softly.

"Of course, but we're always doing this, Ger."

"It's seems that way lately. Do you want to talk?"

Choosing to think she meant they would converse as opposed to talk and to deal directly with the tension that was between them, he proceeded to tell her about Tom Darcy and his unfortunate horse.

"But that's grotesque, grotesque. I've never heard the likes, James. I'm serious. All those years growing up in the country, I thought I'd heard it all. But this?"

"He's very shaken," James added as he agreed.

"It's so awful it strikes me as surely vindictive."

"You think so?"

"Oh most definitely!" Geraldine exclaimed. "It's too vicious. To kill a horse, and in that way!"

"But not necessarily a mind aiming itself at Darcy?"

"I wouldn't be so sure. If it weren't to get at Darcy, then why? Wait!" She stopped suddenly. "Had the horse ever hurt someone?"

"That's a very good question, Ger. What if the horse had a history? If the horse had thrown someone, someone who was badly injured, a child perhaps . . ."

"Yes, that could explain the violence—it could have been a punishing act against the horse."

"But Darcy has owned the horse for years."

"Well there you go! Something tragic happened during those years and he didn't mention it to you."

James looked at Ger thoughtfully, but he realized that he believed that Darcy would have mentioned such a thing to him, would have been completely honest with him.

"Tell me, Ger, what do you know about this man?"

"I know him by reputation of course, and a couple of lectures he gave to us as students since we've been doing our mental health rotation. All that psycho-babble is not for me, even if I am stuck doing it for a while." She stubbed out her cigarette and smiled ironically. "But I do remember him. Some of our lecturers are so dry. Darcy wasn't exactly setting the world on fire, but he struck us as sincere. He came across as caring deeply about his patients. And he's handsome in that kind of low-key way . . ."

"What low-key way?" James bristled with jealousy.

Geraldine laughed and her voice was throaty and warm.

"Oh, James. He's old enough to be my father. He's in his fifties."

Again James bristled, knowing Geraldine was closer to Donald's age than to his own.

"But still has his hair, is that it!"

"Something like that. If you would let me finish, I do remember the theme of his talks. He tried to convince us that patients with psychological problems could be helped by talking. You know, talk therapy. I suppose we all accepted that in a general way. But he did say that one way he could convince his patients to open up was to encourage them to tell him stories."

"Seems simplistic, doesn't it?" James said.

"I suppose so, the way I put it. He presented it in a much more sophisticated way."

The barman approached and James ordered another round and a few packets of crisps and peanuts. A silence grew between them and James began to fidget.

"James," said Geraldine.

"Mmm."

"I thought we came to talk. Are we talking?"

"Of course, we've been talking since we sat down."

"Please don't play games, James," Geraldine

replied, narrowing her eyes as he lit her cigarette.

"Right, what was it we were going to talk about?" His voice was neutral, his lawyerly voice she called it sometimes.

"James, we've known each other a good while now."

"Right."

"And we've gone through some very serious situations together. There was the whole issue of Brona." She paused, her face growing increasingly sad and serious. "And the situation down in Buncloda . . ."

James blushed, ever conscious of how Geraldine had risked her life without knowing it—all to help him solve a troubling case. He felt his face begin to burn.

He nodded, relieved when she didn't continue on that path.

"Look, James, this is difficult for me, too. I have my pride. But since you won't speak and time is passing, I think . . . oh shite."

James jumped. Ger had spilled some of her gin onto her silk dress. She fled to the ladies room to attend to it, and as he waited, he knew he waited with a blank mind.

When she returned, he also knew the mood had changed. She resumed her seat but sat on the edge, gathering her scarf and handbag. "Look, James, it's been a rotten night . . . don't interrupt. I'm determined to say it and I will. The time has come to make a choice: it's Miss Priss or me."

His stomach muscles recoiled as if she had punched him unexpectedly.

He put down his unfinished pint. "Let's call it a night then," he said softly but soberly. They quickly left the pub and drove in silence. She was staying with friends about a quarter of a mile away and he walked her to their gate.

"Good night, James," she said. He hoped to see in her some hint of trepidation, some faint alteration in her tone that would say to him she was nervous, that she feared she'd been too blunt, had gone too far, had not wanted to force him to choose between her and Sarah. But there was none of that.

When he didn't reply immediately, she stood on her toes and kissed him lightly on the cheek. "Must run," she called over her shoulder. Turning on his heel he marched back to the car and drove steadily and angrily home to his bachelor flat.

CHAPTER

7

IT WAS EARLY Friday afternoon when Tom Darcy opened his office door slightly and said softly, "Come, please."

An extremely pale woman in her late twenties walked hesitantly into Tom's office. She was a new patient and he was particularly attentive to all that she did and said.

He indicated the chair opposite his own black leather office chair. She sat at his invitation and placed her purse squarely on her lap.

He noted her thin fingers twining around themselves, the slightly worn cloth coat buttoned to her neck despite the warmth of the day. She remained silent.

"Mrs. Sullivan?"

"Yes," she answered simply, looking at him, clearly waiting for him to take the lead. He sighed inwardly. He sensed already she would be a difficult patient.

"Mrs. Sullivan. Your GP, Dr. Welsh, suggested that you come to see me."

She didn't reply, looking past him toward the bland picture of flowers that hung on the wall, although he suspected that her anxiety was so great that she didn't see the picture itself. It was a place for her eyes to rest.

"Isn't that correct?" Tom insisted.

Her eyes, startled now, flicked back to him.

"Yes," she nearly whispered.

"Dr. Welsh has not informed me of your problem directly. You should understand that what is said here is between us, between you and me."

He waited.

"This is as confidential as it can possibly be," he urged.

"Like confession?" she said, brightening ever so slightly

Tom hesitated. In that split second he experienced doubts, old familiar doubts. Could he give her such a guarantee, knowing as he did the complexities of insurance, of employers' demands, of the vagaries of the legal system. He shut his eyes briefly. Was this in fact what she was asking of him?

"Mrs. Sullivan, I will listen to what you have to tell me. I do not nor should I pass any judgment on you. We are going to share a mutual goal of helping you deal with the events in your life."

He watched her face close over; he could see her shrinking back into her coat.

"I cannot grant you forgiveness."

He watched as she closed her eyes as if against him.

"But I can, together with you, help you to understand . . ."

He hesitated again.

"To understand what it is that is making you feel guilty?" He lifted his voice on the last word. It struck a chord.

She opened her eyes and looked at him. They were glazed as if with tears.

"Are you a medical doctor?"

"Yes," he said simply, having learned years ago to answer only the question asked, as if with a child.

"But you're not a regular doctor?"

"No, I am a psychiatrist. I deal with sickness of the mind, and those of the body which affect the mind. I can prescribe medication, order tests and so on. But I am not a GP and if I find that you have other medical problems I would refer you to your own doctor or to a specialist."

Again he watched her close her eyes as if wrestling with a tough decision. He waited, allowing his compassion for this troubled woman to flow through his mind, through his spirit. He watched the subtle changes of the muscles in her silent face; he noted with an inward sigh the thin hands tightening again on the purse, which she held like a small shield in front of her torso.

She stood slowly, warily, just barely catching his eye.

"Thanks very much," she said quickly in that

rote manner that signaled termination but not gratitude.

"Why don't you think it over, Mrs. Sullivan," he said softly, but when she didn't reply or even look him in the face, he stood and opened the door of his office carefully, checking that no one was waiting. Nor should they have been.

"All right?" he said kindly.

Mrs. Sullivan jumped. "Do I pay you or what?" she said in that frightened manner which had characterized her throughout.

"No, Mrs. Sullivan, not this time. This was a consultation. Your insurance will take care of it. Next time we would need to discuss my fees."

Letting out a suppressed breath, she scurried through the outer door.

There would be no next time, he mused, for Mrs. Sullivan. He was curious as to her problem. He reviewed his own conduct of the interview, jotting his notes on the large lined tablet of paper in front of him on his desk. He placed his half glasses carefully on his nose and began to write as the thoughts flowed into his mind. He always recorded his first impressions of a new patient, in as uncensored a fashion as he could.

His first sense of her, beyond the obvious lack of confidence and the physical signs of depression and nervousness and perhaps limited financial means, was that she was an abused wife. Why? he questioned himself. No bruises, and no information whatsoever. Yet her medical doctor had referred her. And, importantly for a timid person, she'd made the effort to come.

But then that single word: confession. Her conscience was troubled. She'd done something that to her way of thinking was bad. But then why not confess to a priest? He knew that many of his fellow Catholics found great relief in confessing. And some of his patients, too. What could she have been considering telling him and not a priest? Why the concern that he be a medical doctor? Some sexual matter. Some practice, perhaps, that her husband had introduced that struck her as deviant? Even though, in some other marriage, in some other context, it would not be? Can't tell a priest that, or ask him either! Can't tell anyone except a medical doctor, but certainly not the family doctor. Why hadn't Tom met her criteria then?

He sat back and sighed. It wasn't the first time this had happened. He felt an old familiar surge of anger. It certainly would have helped matters if Dr. Welsh, the GP, could have prepared her better. Why let her come to him, only to be confused and embarrassed. She'd not come back nor, Tom suspected, would she go to her priest.

He pictured her as a starving mouse gnawing at its own paw in a spiritual hunger to be reassured. He finished his jottings on that note, and dating the pages, he placed them methodically in a folder and filed it away.

Tom glanced at his diary of appointments for the day ahead. He'd left an hour open for Mrs. Sullivan and now he had some time free before his next client. Mrs. Fogarty had pulled the files on all of his clients for that day and put them in the double drawer of his desk, leaving them in order of their appointments. He took up Mr. Mullins's file and opened it now, staring unseeing for some seconds. Finally he stood up and stretched and then forced himself to sit yet again.

He attempted to focus his mind. He quickly rejected the idea that he was bored. Whatever the outward signs, the cause was not boredom. He loved his work; it could be said he loved his patients, in the true sense of *caritas*. What then was the matter? he questioned himself for the tenth time that day.

Was he burned out? Rashly, as a younger man, he had scoffed at such an idea. The professional journals of the time were fond of discussing the issue. He was eager, fresh; little did he think that the work he had chosen as his life's endeavor could be so draining.

He thought of some of his colleagues: some of them surgeons now, all senior men and consultants. Surely their work was more draining on their mental energies. He'd had this debate with himself more than once.

But was it? He knew they were good to themselves and with that he could not quibble. How sensible of them to golf, to fly off to sunny climates for carefully orchestrated vacation time. Yet he could never justify such vacations to himself or to Joan.

Joan. He'd thought her behavior this morning truly harsh. She hadn't been at all sympathetic over Quixote. He closed his eyes in his continuing resolve not to think about the horse during his working day. He had to keep his mind clear, his spirits steady and even. But Joan was another matter. He tapped his pencil on the folder. He'd made no resolve not to think about her. Or had he? When he did think about her, he reached no conclusions.

Joan had asked for a separation. He knew she was being discreet. What she wanted was a divorce. Her Catholicism would not stand in her way; she'd been fairly lax over the years. Her own laxness had affected him. He'd been going to Mass lately, though, even some early weekday mornings. Now he wondered why. To spite her in some childish way, or to find some solace for himself? He groaned inwardly.

Yes, a separation would in due course lead to a divorce, not easy but now available in Ireland. Selfishly, he wondered what such an outcome would do to his reputation. The patients might never know, he didn't wear a wedding ring as it was. But his colleagues? He imagined them talking about him, ridiculing him—how could he keep someone else's marriage together, if he couldn't manage his own? But that was a good question. If he couldn't work things out with Joan, if they couldn't at least talk things through calmly, what kind of a therapist was he? Tom suddenly felt overwhelmed and distracted.

He was thankful when his thoughts were interrupted by the ring of his desk phone. Mrs. Fogarty had put through a call. He listened as one of his longtime clients spoke of his need to talk with him, and Tom, compassionate as ever, spent the next quarter of an hour in a brief counseling session.

At the appointed time, Tom heard the outer office door open and close. Yes, Mr. Mullins. Tom imagined the ritual unfolding of a newspaper, the paper rustling and whooshing as he pictured Mr. Mullins folding it with mathematical precision. He would run his thumb and middle finger down the folds until they were razor sharp, until the middle column of printed words was smudged and gray patches appeared on the paper and grayer smudges on his fingertips. Tom saw in his mind's eye Mr. Mullins taking out one of his numberless handkerchiefs and rubbing at his ink-stained fingertips. Sweat would be forming on his forehead and soon on his upper lip.

As Tom returned the unread folder to the lower drawer, he glanced at the tiny clock placed strategically on the shelf behind the patient's chair, placed so that he could observe the time without their noticing. Of course some always noticed the momentary flick of his eyes toward the clock. They would register it and stop, however briefly, in mid-sentence, in mid-word. Some clients deliberately moved into awkward positions just to thwart this maneuver. Then he had to resort to his watch. This was a watch he'd found after many trials, with a face and numbers large enough to be read instantly and yet still small enough so that the patient could not read it clearly. He stood up, shook his right leg and then his left to loosen the wrinkles and folds in his trousers. He cleared his throat in an unconscious signal and opened the door.

"Come," he said neutrally.

A shiver of apprehension passed through Mr. Mullins as he stood up, paper clutched nervously but carefully in his hand. Never glancing at Mrs. Fogarty, he entered the office, ducking his head under an imaginary low lintel. He was a tall, gangly man in his late twenties. As he sat in his chair he carefully placed the unread paper on the floor beside him. Not happy with its alignment to the right-hand rung of the chair, he moved it until it was truly parallel.

Without looking at Dr. Darcy he greeted him, took out a clean handkerchief, shook it open from its pristine folds, and mopped his brow, then rubbed the handkerchief across either palm in a futile attempt to absorb the perspiration continuously forming on his hands.

He looked up eventually to see Dr. Darcy sitting opposite him and he felt his tense muscles relax ever so slightly. He studied the doctor's face carefully. He saw him nod encouragingly.

"I don't know where to begin," Mr. Mullins said at last. He glanced down at his lap and immediately remembered the crumpled handkerchief lying there. Startled, he began to fold it along the previously ironed creases. The silence in the room was a warm one. There was little sense of time passing for either man. Unconscious of Tom's patient scrutiny, Mr. Mullins put the now contaminated cloth in his back left trouser pocket and sighed audibly as at a task completed.

Again he looked up. Again Tom nodded.

"It was a pretty good week," Mr. Mullins said at last. He watched as Dr. Darcy raised his eyebrows a fraction.

After a longish pause, Tom said: "Tell me about it then."

Mr. Mullins felt encouraged. No one else in his life ever asked him about his week. A sense of pride filled him and he began haltingly at first and then with a rush.

"Mother was sick this week. She had one of her headaches, you remember the ones I told you about." He looked up quickly from his now empty lap to check that Tom's face registered that memory. It did.

He went on.

"Sometimes they last a day, sometimes a few days, sometimes, a whole week. This week it was a week. In fact, she still had it today and I wasn't sure that I could come today." He hesitated again, and again checked Tom's face.

"But you are here," Tom replied in a neutral tone, nodding once, holding his chin down as his eyes met Mr. Mullins's.

"Yes," he said proudly.

"That's very good, Mr. Mullins."

"Is it? I mean yes, of course." He felt as though he were practicing saying these words; they felt new and a bit strange. To be making a statement instead of asking a question.

"Yes, it is good."

Suddenly Mr. Mullins leapt from his chair. Tom maintained his posture, seemingly unruffled. Mr. Mullins noticed that. He noticed all such things. Tom didn't flinch. That was good. That was very good.

As abruptly he sat down.

"No, it's not," he said in a low voice, in fact so low it was inaudible. He didn't know that it was so.

"Pardon me?" Tom asked.

"You heard me," Mr. Mullins answered more loudly.

Tom remained silent.

"I said, no it's not good, not good. In fact, not good at all."

"Why is it not good?"

There was a ringing sound in Mullins's ears. He would have to tell, yes. He would. Have to. Tell his mother. He could feel the pressure mounting. He felt the wetness on his lip. Mother hated his sweat. He was sweating today. She had seen it. She didn't believe his lie when he said he wanted to go to the bookie. Just a flutter, he'd said. What would you know of flutters, or betting, or any of those hideous male habits. Habits. She'd like him to have nice habits. Or was that hobbies. He looked up suddenly. Dr. Darcy was studying his fingernails, one hand resting at ease on the other. No, Darcy didn't sweat, he probably never sweat.

"You don't sweat," he said, just then hearing his voice speaking aloud. This habit also bothered people, Mother said. Speaking up, out of turn, she said. Or was it out of tune?

He remembered he'd said something to Dr. Darcy, but Tom's face was impassive. Had he heard him? Was he ignoring him? This made him angry. Dr. Darcy knew that.

"Sweating isn't good," he blurted out.

"I don't know about that, Mr. Mullins," Tom replied conversationally. "Sweating is neither good nor bad," he added after a brief pause. "People perspire, it's a biological fact. When they exercise, or work hard physically, or sometimes when they are a little nervous."

Mr. Mullins felt riled. "I am not nervous," he said defiantly.

"But I think you're working very hard," Tom replied softly. "You've been working very hard when you come here. We've been working hard together."

Mr. Mullins felt the tension ease for a second time. He leaned back in his chair. He smiled in agreement with this statement.

"Why don't you tell me what happened before you came here today."

Mr. Mullins studied his blue, wool-clad knees.

"I told Mother I was going to a bookie to lay a bet."

"And?"

"She didn't believe me." He glared at Tom. "She knew I was lying."

"How did she know that?"

"She knows, she always knows, she always did know. And then the sweat starts coming." Unconsciously Mr. Mullins touched his upper lip.

"So, you think she knows you're not being direct with her." Tom paused.

"When I sweat. Sweat—that's the problem. I've

said that from the beginning." He knew he had. That's why he'd come here over a year ago. Old Dr. Brennan made him come. He'd tell his mother if he didn't. But his mother didn't know. Mr. Mullins shook his head to clear the fog that was building up.

"I think we talked about this before," he heard Tom say patiently. "Haven't we?"

Mr. Mullins looked at Tom's kind expression.

He shrugged.

"Yes, I suppose we have."

"The sweating perhaps is something that bothers you, Mr. Mullins, but didn't we agree that it was your idea of what other people make of it that is the heart of what we've been working on?"

"Yes."

"Do you think that your mother knows that you come here?"

"Yes, I mean, no." He shrugged again. "She doesn't believe in all this, you see." Mr. Mullins extracted another fresh handkerchief from his pocket.

Tom nodded.

"Do you?"

"Yes."

"That's what matters."

"I did try to tell her. But it was that headache, you see."

"It's interesting you said you were going to lay a bet, Mr. Mullins. Just to be clear now, did you in fact go into a bookie's on your way here?"

Mr. Mullins jumped. "Actually, I tried. When I got off the bus, well, I suppose you know there's a bookie just down the road in the row of shops there?"

Tom was impassive.

"I went towards the front. I even looked through the door; it was propped open. But it was jammed with people, with men. And, well, I stepped in but it was noisy and confusing. Names and numbers and some windows at the back, two with men behind them. I couldn't see what to do so . . ." He felt the color drain from his face, the strength from his muscles.

"That's good, that's very good. Now, this is what I would like you to try. On your way back to the bus, go into the bookie's, go to the window in the back, put a pound coin on the counter, and say you want the favorite in the next race. The clerk will do the rest. Just answer any questions he asks you."

Mr. Mullins felt the trembling begin. It started where it always started, in his calves. Even though he was sitting he could feel it working its way up his legs until the thigh muscles began to quiver. He slapped his hands on to his thighs but then they too began to shake.

"No," he managed to say from the back of his parched throat.

"You can do it."

Mr. Mullins shook his head.

"Why?"

"Because they'll know, they'll all know."

"Who will know?"

"The people."

"What people?"

"The men."

"What will they know?"

"They'll know that I don't know what to do."

"They might. But they don't know you."

He heard Tom stress the last word.

"You can do this. I've told you what to do. No one will notice you however, because no one knows you."

The trembling was easing. He could lie to Dr. Darcy as well as he could lie to his mother. Yes, he'd agree. It was so simple. He'd just agree and Dr. Darcy would stop talking. But he didn't feel his muscles relax for a third time.

"All right. I'll do it," Mr. Mullins agreed. Then, strengthening his voice, he repeated the phrase.

"Good." Tom went on to allay Mr. Mullins's fears in a number of ways, reinforcing what would be new and brave behavior for him. Finally he ended with his customary phrase: "Now, our time is about up," and he stood up slowly.

Mr. Mullins also stood. He felt a little dizzy as he reached into his pocket and took out the cash he had prepared on the bus. It was in a small brown envelope. He placed it on Dr. Darcy's desk.

"Thank you, Doctor."

"Thank you, Mr. Mullins," Tom said.

Mr. Mullins felt the doctor's eyes riveted on his upper lip. He felt the sweat beading on his skin. He felt the beads of sweat growing, swelling into enormous droplets, falling now from his face past his elongated dizzy body to the pale carpet below. But his vision was blurred. He couldn't see the spots of water on the brown carpeting, but he knew they were there. He saw the white oblong on the floor, and sitting down briefly on the edge of the chair, he reached for his paper. He stood up and as Dr. Darcy murmured good-bye he walked unsteadily through the door and then somehow through the outer office door. He walked robotically down the short corridor, turning left with precision, and continued down the short flight of stairs to the heavier double-glazed glass door. Leaning on the steel crossbar, he pushed open the outside door, gulping for air as he did so. The bus stop looked many miles away in the glimmering sunlight.

The shops were there too, and he walked unsteadily closer. Maybe. Just maybe. He could hear Dr. Darcy's kind, firm voice inside his head. "You can do it, Mr. Mullins," he heard him saying. Dr. Darcy would be pleased, really pleased. Mullins looked in the door of the bookie's. It was dark, but there weren't many people at all. With all his strength he lifted his left foot over the low threshold and stepped in, his eyes fixed on the desk. Dr. Darcy would be proud of him.

CHAPTER
—— 8 ——

Tom smiled as he sat back and jotted his case notes into Mr. Mullins's folder. He had a fondness for him despite the fact he could be so exasperating. Progress was slow, very slow, but it was progress. As Tom stood and stretched, releasing the tension in his neck and back, he heard the waiting room door open and shut. He smiled again. It was Emily, admittedly his favorite patient.

Conscious of his own vanity, he withdrew a small bottle of cologne from the side drawer of his desk and splashed a bit onto his face, patting it briskly but quietly. Despite the absence of a mirror, he smoothed back his hair and straightened his tie. With a quick glance at his notes to remind himself of the last few minutes of their previous meeting, he composed himself. And with a serious expression he opened the door to the waiting room. Standing slightly to one side, he leaned his head out and said, "Come," quite distinctly to the floor.

Emily stood and smiled a quick flashing smile. He was used to her ways now, her shyness and her reserve, but it had taken a good while at the beginning of her therapy two years before. Now as she sat and talked, he listened, not so much to the content of what she was telling him, the overt events of her week as a young lecturer at the university, a very intelligent woman without any close relatives, who lived alone. Somewhere he registered the information, but he was caught as always by her gentle demeanor, her body language, unconsciously sexual. Her voice, always soft, was as melodious as ever. He liked to listen to her voice.

Emily Lawlor was well dressed today, he noted, and well groomed—signs that she was feeling more confident. Her golden brown hair, recently trimmed, shone in the artificial light of the room. He liked the way it fell forward as she moved her head, little wisps of gold clinging sometimes to her cheeks. He crossed his legs to settle into a more comfortable position and noted wryly that only seconds later she crossed her legs in the same position. So unconscious was their communication that she had no idea that she had done so. This unspoken link touched him, and today, somehow especially today, he just wanted to hear her softly talking to him and only to him, needing him, leaning on him. The black dress she wore he had seen before. She looked very well in it in a sort of bohemian way. He liked the way the wide neck of the dress would slip to one side, making her appear fragile, delicate, despite her height.

Tom pulled himself back from his wandering. She had stopped talking and was looking at him expectantly. Fortunately he had been listening to her at some level, and catching her glance, he looked beyond her at the wall.

"Let me see," he said neutrally, "I hear you saying that it was a good week for you. That you felt stronger in yourself standing in front of your class, and that some of your symptoms have, let's say, abated."

He watched as her face brightened. She didn't ever quite smile but her expression would open, her eyes light up, her eyebrows would lift into an expression of delight and confidence. It pleased him whenever a patient would show such a response to his words. But with Emily, it was infinitely more satisfying. Her expression was so sensitive, so intelligent, her eyes quick to catch his at times, in understanding, in insight. Not conventionally pretty, it was at those times she struck him as quite beautiful. And somehow virginal. As indeed she was.

He tried to focus on what she was saying.

"Oh, yes, that's very true. It was a good week. In fact," she rushed on, the words tumbling out, "not only did I feel it each day, but from class to class. I've been less self-conscious, more at ease, sometimes, I might say, even in command." She laughed ironically.

Tom Darcy nodded, smiling his acknowledgment of her sense of her own progress.

"Good, good," he was saying in gestures. This had been so hard to learn at first. It had taken him years to move away from the conventional practice of his art: listening impassively; taking medical histories, family histories, jotting notes throughout his sessions. He'd even, for a while, tried using a tape recorder—much to his patients' total intimidation. They left him—some physically; others, too polite to leave, instead dried up before his eyes. He had in time learned to respond to his patients, to support them, to understand their needs. He mused along to himself, at one level listening to Emily recount how the flutters in her stomach had stopped and how the dryness of her mouth was easing with each class; at another, listening for the hidden meaning behind her words.

"And the students laughed at my joke, it wasn't a great joke..." she was saying deprecatingly, "but..."

He cut across her habitual downplaying of even her small successes. "Tell me the joke," he said gently, but smiling broadly.

"Oh, no, I couldn't." Emily began to shift uneasily in her chair. Her hands, which had been fluttering like delicate white birds, gripped the arms of the chair. Unaware, she began to pick at the fabric, just slightly, because even in her confusion her body language was controlled.

"Don't pick," he could hear the critical mother saying.

"Don't fidget so," he could hear the deceased father saying, as clearly as if he were in the room, to the only daughter, the only child of elderly parents. Don't ever leave us, no, it's your duty to stay at home. No boyfriend is good enough. After all, sex is dirty, meaningless, mindless. The ridicule of her appearance, her voice, her clothes. Punishments and deprivations. Demeaning her personality, her very occupation. So much loneliness. So much repression. Tom sighed to himself.

"It wasn't very good, really. I seem to have forgotten how it went." Emily looked down at the floor and then up at the wall behind him.

He let the silence hang in the room, with mixed feelings. He'd thought it a good choice for him, for her, to make a small request for her to act in a social way with him, in the endless reparative work which he did with her. But clearly it was a bigger task than he'd realized. Just to repeat a simple joke to him was growing in her mind, he realized now, into an intolerable scene of potential humiliation. She would perceive it somewhere inside as pressure, her old deep-seated reactions still on a hair trigger.

She shifted again, and then assumed a terrible stillness of body if not of mind. Her head was down, cowed. Anger flowed through him and as quickly left him.

"Tell me what you are feeling now," he whispered into the heavy silence he had inadvertently generated between them.

"What I'm feeling? Well . . ." There was a long pause as she struggled to say the words.

"Yes, just that."

"I am feeling quite small, and foolish, and I'm

sorry I opened my mouth." She looked up angrily, but that too vanished. "I am feeling that I sidetracked this session with my stupid petty little joke."

"Tell me why you feel foolish?"

He waited, hoping this now painful situation would trigger memories in Emily that she would share, and in the sharing he could begin to fit the pieces together for her. There were so many pieces.

"I remember when I was little." She looked at him for confirmation.

He merely acknowledged she had spoken.

"I used to learn silly little jokes, oh you know what I mean. What did the big chimney say to the little chimney . . ." Again she looked at him. Tom noticed with each glance that she grew more timid, less forthright.

"Such as?" he urged.

"One I recall was, um." She hesitated. "What do you get when you mix a kangaroo and a sheep?" He watched the flush creep up her delicate neck.

"I don't know, what?" said Tom honestly.

"A woolly jumper." Emily laughed as Tom reacted, laughing too.

"I'll have to remember that. I am hopeless for remembering jokes."

She looked up again, less timid, her face full of gratitude.

"I don't think that was the joke you told your class at the university, however," Tom pressed on.

"No, it wasn't," she said, smiling. "Do you really want to hear that one?" She was relaxing again, her hands once again animated. She looked up, unconsciously taking a breath.

"What does an insomniac, dyslexic, agnostic do?"

Tom was thoughtful. This one was new to him.

At last he nodded as if to say, go on.

Again she paused, then, smiling, giving herself away, said, "He stays awake all night trying to figure out if there really is a dog."

As Tom got the joke he laughed heartily, genuinely amused, and Emily too laughed. Relaxing, unconsciously she moved her seat nearer to him. Suddenly Tom was excruciatingly aware of her physical presence. He too shifted in his chair, crossing his legs again, accidentally tipping her shoe with his own. As a therapist he knew instantly he was reacting to her in a sexual way. As a man he knew too that he wanted her, then and there, physically, and that his attempt to master his desire was a feeble one. Half horrified, half relieved to give in, he allowed his fantasy to stay in his mind.

"Sorry," they each said simultaneously. She blushed again and he felt the heat rise to his face.

"I have to tell you," she said with great hesitancy, not looking at him now.

"What?" he whispered, his voice hoarse and low, his heart racing uncharacteristically.

"I think I've fallen in love with you . . ."

"I see."

"I've been wanting to tell you for some time, and fighting it, all at the same time."

"Go on."

"I know it's not right."

"Why do you say that?"

"It's obvious—you're married."

"In this room there are just the two of us—"

"Please, you've explained that—that I can have any feeling—hate, love, rage, despair—and express it here safely. That what I say isn't right or wrong." She paused, still without looking up at him.

"This is different," she said at last. "This isn't therapy now. This isn't something to analyze." Tears dropped on her hands. "I want more. I want to see you outside this room. I want to take walks with you. Oh, I see things in shops, like beautiful sweaters and other presents I want to buy for you. I want to sit with you . . ."

"When?"

"At the end of the day."

"At the end of the day," he repeated softly.

"Yes, and we'd sit, and we'd tell each other about how our day had gone, what had happened. We'd put our feet up and talk and talk . . ."

"Anything else?" His heart seemed to stop as he waited to hear what he truly wanted her to say, then and there no longer the professional listening to a patient, but a man—vulnerable, aroused, lost.

"Yes, but I can't say it."

"Try, please." How many times had he said this to patients? It was familiar to him, familiar to her. He knew she would try, she would try because he had asked her to. But he knew this time he wasn't asking her for professional reasons.

"I want you to love me," Emily said at last with great effort.

"Go to bed with you?" Darcy bit his lip.

"Yes."

There was a terrible silence in the room.

"I can't," Tom said at last. "As a lover I'd make a terrible therapist," he added. He closed his eyes briefly. What had he done? Rage at his own glibness surged through his mind. He'd brought her to the point of confessing such feelings, he'd used his therapy techniques for selfish ends, and then he had retreated, falling back on stock phrases. He felt shame move through him and he loosened his collar.

Silently, he watched as she reached for her things, her vision blurred with tears. She stood up without looking at him, but with some newly awakened dignity. He too stood and walked, as he always did, to the door to open it for her. As she passed him, again without looking at him, her hand inadvertently brushed against his suit jacket and he shivered to his soul.

"Have a good week, Emily," he said as if by rote.

"Oh, please," she said bitterly, head down. "How can you be so cruel?" She looked at him suddenly. "I trusted you, Tom, and I loved you beyond life itself." She turned then and walked quickly from the office.

CHAPTER
9

ELIZABETH, FOR THAT'S how Tom knew her, was Tom's most troubling client. She had come to him by a circuitous route. He'd heard of her case some years before. She had been a young woman, of twenty years of age and married to a lad in the country, when she had murdered her mother-in-law, had stabbed her quite unexpectedly one sunny morning in the kitchen of her little flat a few days after the birth of her first child.

At the time he'd been intrigued by the scenario and frustrated by the lack of cogent details in the papers. Although charges were brought by the police, she had been freed under the influence of an old law which held that a postpartum mother was not legally responsible for her actions for some number of days after the delivery of her child.

Tom had read of the early history of the English law that had developed as a result of the hundreds of cases of young unmarried women who had committed infanticide in the nineteenth century. The girls involved had been in service, country girls, many of them Irish girls, who were housemaids in the great, and not so great, houses of England. Unwed mothers totally dependant on their meager positions, these girls had often been driven to smother the children at their secret births and then continue on in their jobs. Many of the fathers had been the men of the households, the fathers and sons of the richer classes. The law for once seemed to have pity and claimed for these young women that they were not responsible. Of course, Tom had noted ironically, it had also kept a lot of well-known names out of the papers, if the girls had been asked to name the fathers of their out-of-wedlock children.

This case was different, of course. The young woman had delivered under normal circumstances. She was married and her husband was at work at the time of the killing, which meant he had a job. What then had snapped?

After the court case, the couple had moved to Dublin to escape the scandal of their life in the smaller country town. They'd altered their names and seemed to be trying to resume their lives. And now, after such a circuitous route, she was coming for therapy with Dr. Darcy.

Elizabeth entered his office as she had since they'd begun work five months before. Fortunately he'd had time to take a break between Emily's appointment and this one, and he had attempted, successfully he believed, to reestablish his professional calm and distance.

When Emily had left Tom had been full of a terrible regret and self-criticism. He'd analyzed what had happened, realizing that his situation with Joan had made him vulnerable to his fantasies about Emily. It was difficult for a man and a woman, who became attracted to each other for whatever complex reasons, to meet week after week, closeted in a small room, talking. One was stripping away layer after layer of his or her personal life, naked for the other to see. The other person, in this case himself, was listening, caring for, sometimes even loving that person. What other professional situation put two people so close together for such intense periods? Tom prayed that Emily would come back so that he could attempt to repair the damage he'd done. And desperately gleaning some good result out of his error, he told himself that he would use this as a caution to himself as a professional. Thus he focused even more intently on the patient in front of him.

Elizabeth threw herself into the chair opposite him and as usual began to fiddle with whatever it was she was holding; this day it was a covered cup of coffee from the local café down the road. She placed it on the corner of his desk and proceeded with disregard to take off the lid, scattering drops onto the surface. Tom closed his eyes briefly in an expression of disapproval but she carried on. She puffed and blew and waved her hand over the rising steam, finally taking a sip and exclaiming that it had burned her mouth.

She put the cup down and took out a stick of chewing gum and proceeded to chew it, snapping it loudly at fanatically regular intervals. Tom strained to overlook the provocation of these movements with professional patience if not genuine virtue.

"Hello, Elizabeth," he said, knowing that she would not begin on her own.

"Hi," she said, drawling it out in what she thought was an American accent. He knew that she watched much television, and attributed some of her superficial presentation to what she observed on the telly.

"How was your week?" he asked noncommittally.

"It sucked," she snapped, not looking at him. "Every week it sucks, and every week I tell you the same thing."

Tom waited. And waited. He recognized they were at an impasse. At no time in the five months of erratic interviews had she cooperated in the therapeutic relationship. He felt, as was usual when he was with her, like a strict schoolteacher dealing with a stubborn, rebellious child.

"You know, Elizabeth, we have to try to work together. I can't do the work on my own, and you can't. In this situation we have to, well, open ourselves up to each other, get to know each other in a deeper sense."

"Yeah, right," she snapped again, the Americanism grating on his ears. "I know nothin' about you, but I'm supposed to pour out my heart and soul to you." Her voice was strident and, he observed, tired.

"You know what you need to know about me," Tom repeated patiently. "I'm your therapist, I am trained in this work, I've helped many people over the years."

"Are you married?" Elizabeth looked at him boldly.

"Yes." He decided to share something with her, to make consciously a swap for something about her. "And you too are married."

She tossed her head. Despite her stubbornness and her challenges, he knew this particular question about him had to be significant.

"Why don't you ever talk about it then? What's she like, the wife?"

Tom merely shook his head, indicating that yet again he would not talk about his personal life.

"All right, all right." Elizabeth sagged in her chair. "You're not going to tell me. But I can guess. She's perfect, right?" Her eyes scanned his face for a reaction but there was none.

"Why do you think my wife, or my life, for that matter, is perfect?" he asked, pushing hard this time.

"I can tell."

"Then tell me how," he urged.

"I bet you have kids, a boy and a girl. They're perfect little pricks too."

"Too?"

"Yeah, just like you. And your wife. Perfect."

"Perfect, how?"

"Lookin' down on the rest of us, that's how. I

can just see you four snob pricks in your perfect
semi-d. Everyone dressed perfect, everyone doing
everything just perfect."

Tom knew she was describing a fantasy, but a
very important one. He tried carefully, not wanting to interrupt the flow.

"So my kids are perfect?"

"See? I knew there were kids."

He made a mental note of his own slip.

"All right," he said softly. "Tell me why that
annoys you."

"What?"

"You seem to be annoyed that I am perfect,
with a perfect life."

"I don't give a bloody damn about your life. It's
my life I'm here to talk about. You told me that
over and over again. Ask me about that, why
don't you?"

"Why don't you just tell me what you want
to . . . about your life." Tom's voice was firm as
the girl before him, with her unattractive greasy
hair, her gum-snapping, her cheap earrings and
the cheap-looking but real leather jacket, threw
her head in her hands and burst into tears.

He let her cry it out, pushing the box of tissues
closer to her on the desk. The cup of coffee stood
there, the milk congealing on the cooling surface.
She grabbed the tissues without looking up and
blew loudly into a handful of them.

"Talk to me, Elizabeth. Please, tell me what
you are feeling . . ."

"Why, why do want to, to listen to me . . . ?"
Her voice was high and shrill, full of suspicion.

"Because that's what I do," Tom said simply.

Elizabeth heaved an enormous sigh from the depths of her fatigue. "How can I trust you?" she said softly.

Tom didn't answer. He never did know how to answer this question that so many of his patients had asked him over the years.

He had had some clients that had never asked. It seemed that they just knew. How weak an explanation that was, he had mused then, as he mused now. Elizabeth was not talking; she sipped the cold coffee and tried to calm the dry sobs that shook her still. Yes, there had been some patients who had just accepted that he cared for them. He'd learned, when others had asked more directly, as Elizabeth did now, not to tell them that he cared about them, about their lives, the suffering their illnesses brought them, their sometimes terrible psychological pain. He'd learned the hard way that Irish people did not want to hear such empathy expressed openly.

Once, early in his practice, he told a lonely, gruff, old and hardened Dublin shopkeeper with a drinking problem that he cared for him. The man simply stood up and left.

They might not want to hear it said, but they did need to hear it. He believed that. As he would need to hear it said. As he admitted, now, suddenly, that he wanted to hear it said to him. By Emily? By Joan? By someone. He shut his eyes against the overwhelming blackness that he sensed was welling up inside. The old familiar wave of loneliness. Or was it? Perhaps it was flowing from Elizabeth, who was sitting opposite him all this time, staring blankly, desperately, into space.

"Elizabeth." He paused as she lifted her exhausted face to his. All defiance was gone. The vulnerability of the unattractive girl before him, with her black eye makeup streaked across her face, her nose red from crying, her cheeks stained with dried tears, moved him beyond measure.

"Elizabeth, talk to me. I am not perfect. My life is not perfect. No one's is. We are all a part of this human race. Some of us have more trouble than others, you know that. I try to help people, that's all. I try, and sometimes I succeed. Tell me, please. I won't . . ." he sought for just the right word. "I won't . . . criticize you."

She smiled for the first time in five months. "I know you won't," she said directly, and he knew what a breakthrough they had made.

"Good," he said in his normal voice, firm and rich and strong, infinitely reassuring to his patients.

Elizabeth sighed deeply, almost shuddering with the force of the air being expelled from her body.

"She did, you see." Scorn filled her voice, and hatred too.

"All the time," Elizabeth continued. "From before we got married. She worked in their shop in our town. I'd go in there with my friends, when we were off the bus after school. You know the way. As soon as we were on the bus, we'd loosen those bloody stupid school uniforms, they were navy."

She mused, looking inward. Tom knew she could see exactly what she was recounting to him now in her mind's eye, and he was pleased.

"I'd have the tie one way, hanging off. The school always said they'd know if we actually took them off. And we'd pull out our blouses so they'd hang out over the skirts and then we'd roll up the skirts at our waists to make them shorter. We'd go in the shop and buy crisps and sweets and generally mess about, shrieking and screaming after being in school all day. She'd watch us. Who did she think she was anyway?"

"I don't know, unless you can tell me," Tom said softly, willing her on.

"I'll tell you—the bitch thought she was the bee's knees. She worked in the shop, so what? I knew I was going to do better than that. I was going to get out of that town. There's nothing there, you know." Elizabeth spoke rhetorically and he said nothing.

"She'd pick on all of us, with her 'oh, and girls in my day' shite. So we'd do things to get at her. Well, at least I did, and some of the others. Jeannie and myself, we were the worst. But it was only a bit of fun. She never forgot that though. Always bringing it up after we got married . . ."

"Bringing up what?"

"How I was cheap even when I was in school."

"Cheap?"

"Well, it only just confirmed what she thought, didn't it?" She looked at Tom angrily.

"Confirmed what?"

"That we had to get married, as they say. We didn't have to get married!" she cried out suddenly, passionately. "We wanted to. Ciaran and I wanted to get married. We would have got married even if we hadn't got pregnant. But she blamed me for that too, but I told her that it takes two to tango."

Tom smiled slightly and Elizabeth relaxed.

She grew pensive and he shifted in his chair.

"What? Is my time up!" she exclaimed bitterly.

Tom was always amazed at the quickness of her perceptions—the slightest change in his demeanor, in the tension in the room, in sounds outside the room. He recognized her heightened state.

"No, our time is not up." But he knew it was growing close.

"Go on," he said in a tone of voice that intimated that he had hours, days, ahead of him, devoted entirely to hearing her story.

She remained quiet.

Tom tried to sum up in his mind what work had been done today. He wanted her to be able to pick up next week with this level of openness and perhaps insight.

"It seems to me," he said slowly, watching her face, "that here was a significant adult in your life, a married woman who had a job, and who worked together with her husband to keep that shop going, to support their family and . . ."

"That's true," she interrupted. "There was Ciaran and his older sister. All brought up with that shop."

"Your future mother-in-law was probably very hard on herself . . . and on other people?"

He let the question hang and she nodded.

"She had no time for frivolous things, nose to the grindstone, that sort of person?"

Again she nodded.

"Perhaps she held other people to her own standards. Especially you, Elizabeth, coming in from outside the family circle, a young woman but nonetheless a woman. Perhaps you were drawing her son out of and away from that tight circle of hard work and family togetherness?"

"Oh yeah, I told you how the sister worked in the shop too." Elizabeth's expression brightened as Tom drew an accurate picture for her of this family he'd never met.

"She was hard on you . . . She wanted everything to be perfect for him. Perhaps she thought that only she could make everything perfect for him?"

"That's right!" Elizabeth cried.

"And you went along with that in your heart. You wanted everything to be perfect too."

Elizabeth looked stunned. Tom watched closely as a range of expressions crossed her face.

"Yes, I did. I wanted everything to be perfect. I was going to show that bitch I was as good as she was. And it was perfect. We rented two rooms in her house, at the top. I didn't like that part. She was always up there visiting, as she called it. Snooping is what it really was. She'd come in when I wasn't there. I wanted to find a place of our own, but well, that town is very small . . ." She stared off as if seeing it all before her.

"We had a few nice pieces, a three-piece suite and a lovely kitchen table. I cleaned and washed

and the windows were clean, and the floor too.
Hell, I didn't have much else to do. The kitchen
was tiny! I'd left school. She didn't want me to
help in the shop, the bloody endless shop! But he
was there morning, noon, and night. And . . ."

"And you were at home, upstairs, by yourself?"

"Yes, the girls I knew, they went off to college
or training schemes or whatever. I was the only
fool who got pregnant that year."

Tom waited, unsure which line to help her
pursue, searching for the key.

"But you had a husband."

He saw a flicker of a smile.

"And a baby on the way," he added.

Her face hardened. "I did everything right.
But she was on me every minute. Drink milk;
don't gain weight. Exercise; rest. Don't be lazy;
put your feet up. Ahh! Orders, orders. She had
me demented. Don't smoke, don't eat. I just carried on. I saw the doctor, I knew I was healthy
and strong. When the baby began to move I was
thrilled, and Ciaran was excited. He never took
much of an interest day to day, but he let me
have my way. I learned to make little matinee
jackets from a woman in the town, in yellow and
green—baby colors. Before I got too big I
painted our room all white, semigloss paint, too.
I made new curtains. I got a Moses basket from
one of the older married women in the town and
made the liner for that too. I got everything
ready."

Tears welled up in her eyes and fell onto her
hands and her lap. Tears burned in Tom's eyes

but he knew after all these years that they would not fall.

The silence was heavy and the room grew hot.

"How is the baby?"

"Oh, she's grand, grand." Elizabeth brushed the tears away.

"Did your mother-in-law like the baby?"

Elizabeth shook her head violently. "Of course not. She never came to the hospital. And when we brought the baby home, she came upstairs and just glanced at her, saying she looked like me—real nasty like. She didn't even like her name."

"What is her name?"

"Tiffany."

Tom was struck by the name. The name of a famous New York store, he thought; the name of a lampshade, as many people assumed; the title of a movie he had liked once because Audrey Hepburn was so pretty. It was a name that was seemingly remote from Irish life, from this girl sitting before him. Certainly it was remote from that woman in a small Irish town who worked all her life to keep a home, to raise her children, to run her shop. The respectable woman who attended church, attended to all her duties. A harsh woman perhaps, not a loving woman, but a woman driven by a sense of responsibility and respectability. What anger she must have felt toward this girl, nothing like herself, intruding into her life, her family. A harsh, cold, unforgiving woman perhaps. He would never know now.

"How did you feel when you came home from hospital?" he asked.

"I was grand at first. It was like playing with a doll. My mother rang and my dad sent flowers. They didn't visit. My brother in Dublin sent money in a card. I nearly died with the thrill of that! He was nineteen and never paid any attention to me before. The baby had come a little early and I hadn't got a pram, but we were waiting on one from one of my cousins in Galway. My mother rang every day. She was going to come the following week to visit. She said she felt funny, you know, visiting me at that house. She didn't want to put a foot wrong. She and the other one never spoke after I found out I was pregnant. Mam even went to a different Mass so as not to see her there at church."

Elizabeth slumped in the chair, exhaustion all over her face and body. Tom glanced quickly at his clock. Their time was surely up and he knew his next patient was waiting, having heard the telltale click of the door. He tried to gauge if Elizabeth had gone as far as she could and if it would help her to stop her at this point. And yet could they recapture this momentum after a week had passed? He waited, hoping her next words would guide him.

"Do you want to talk about that day, Elizabeth?" He looked at her openly, compassion in his face.

She looked up and stared, sighing. "No, not today."

"Well then, our time is up for today."

He knew instantly he'd said the wrong thing and mentally kicked himself. He'd rushed her and she'd reacted immediately. He watched, rather sadly, as she smoothed her face with her hands, as if putting on a mask. She shook out her hair over her shoulders and straightened her jacket. Standing up, she pointed angrily at the clock.

"Gave me a big extra five minutes, Doctor, didn't you? I don't know if the Eastern Health Board will pay you for that!" She swung around toward him, tears in her eyes.

"I don't understand. I don't understand you, or this, any of this . . ." She waved her hands wildly, indicating Tom and the office at once. "Why do you do this to me? It's torture, that's what it is. Torture. You get me to remember, to talk about it, to relive it for God's sake! And then you have the almighty goddamned nerve to tell me the time is up! Time is up!"

She leaned over him, nearly breathless.

"Do you know what it is like to live with this every hour of the day? Do you think the time is ever up for me? You think I can switch it on and off, just for you, just when I am here!" Elizabeth was screaming now. "I killed my husband's mother—don't you think I see it in his eyes every day? I killed my baby's granny! And you sit there, you smug, self-satisfied bastard, and coax me to talk about it all in that frigging soft voice of yours. Well, not anymore. I don't care what the courts or you or anybody tells me. I'll see you in hell before I'll ever see you in this office again!"

She flung herself toward the door and slammed it behind her.

Tom, exhausted but pleased to some degree, sat back in his chair. Although he had unintentionally provoked it, her angry outburst could be a sign of healthy progress. Experienced as he was, he believed she would return, and next time, he resolved, he would be more careful.

CHAPTER
—10—

JAMES WORKED OVER the next few days in pur-
suit of the Darcy case. He surprised himself with
his zealousness and wondered why he had taken
to Darcy the way he had. Of course, there was
always Maggie as motivator, with her very high
opinion of the medical profession and her rather
low opinion of his own.

"Any news yet?" she demanded as he rose
from his desk in the inner office and came out to
stretch his legs and make some coffee in hers.

"I'm afraid not," he answered, embarrassed
that he had nothing to tell her.

"I assume you read Dave Whelan's report?" she
called to him from her computer terminal.

Dave Whelan was a retired police officer
who'd been injured on the job. It had happened
on a dark night in a county to the northwest;
Dave had always remained vague on that point.
He and his fellow gardai had been scouring the

local fields for a suspect in a rural murder and
arson job. Dave had fallen into a ditch separating
two fields, a deep ditch as luck, or misfortune,
would have it, and he had badly broken his leg
and subsequently suffered numerous complica-
tions. Only in his late forties, he moved and
spoke like a man much older. But he did excellent confidential investigative work and James
had used him on many occasions.

"Of course I read it. None too helpful, as I'm
sure you already know."

"Indeed, I typed it for him . . . in my off time,
James," she replied as James raised a quizzical
and very black eyebrow in her direction.

"The previous owners are still happily settled in
Brockville, apparently a lovely town in Ontario. So
much so, they haven't been back here for a visit."

"Hardly surprising," said James, "it's only four
years and the wife is Canadian."

"Humph," was Maggie's only reply.

"After all this time, Maggie, you can't just suspect everyone. It shows a lack of faith and trust
in your fellow man—men—people," James strove
to correct his seemingly chauvinistic mistake.

"It just would have made some kind of sense,"
she said petulantly, her frustration showing.

"I agree. At this point this crime seems pointless. By the way, I've spent some time with Mrs.
Killian."

"Oh, I'm sure," Maggie interrupted with sarcasm. "All you Prods know how to ride."

"I don't know about all of us," said James,
stung yet again, "but I do. And yes, I did go rid-

ing. I'd been to that stable before. Mrs. Killian strikes me as above suspicion. Apart from anything else, what would she have to gain? The death of the horse represents a loss to her, of the stable fees at the very least, and of Darcy's goodwill, and that of any of his friends. And a necropsy is very dear. And all of it is bad publicity for her stables. I've talked to a lot of the stable hands as well."

"But not all?"

"No, but I'll be going back. You know, Maggie, it's the lack of motive that puzzles me. If I could just get a handle on that."

"Well there is always just pure badness," said Maggie as she switched off the screen of her computer.

"Okay, perhaps it was just pure badness, as you say. Perhaps any horse would have done, to a mind bent on destroying an animal. And perhaps it just happened to be Darcy's. Perhaps that's all there is to it—horrible but true. But it's hard to understand—the supposed satisfaction to that kind of mind of killing something beautiful." James shrugged eloquently.

"Like the way those bloody vandals knock all the heads off the tulips in Stephens Green?" Maggie picked up her small elegant handbag.

"Look, I'm not going out. I'll do some work here, if you'd bring me back a kebab or a gyro or something I could eat at my desk?"

"Right, I'll pick up something nice for you, but it'll be an hour or so." She smiled her usual defiant smile, challenging him to tell her to be back on time. But he didn't and she knew he wouldn't, not in his present frame of mind. "Good luck," she said as she left.

James stretched out on the sofa in his office and gazed through the tall Georgian windows toward the tops of the trees and the blue sky above them, his mind's eye seeing Darcy's troubled face. Although now inclined to think it was a motiveless crime, something still nagged him. He allowed his mind to drift, images floating into his consciousness unbidden. The killing of the horse was so striking in its viciousness. He thought of the police photos of the scene that he'd viewed at the station. The horse's beautiful head, the curve of the once powerful neck, the vast crimson-black pool of blood. No, he thought, decisively this time, there was indeed a motive. There was only one motive that could account for this killing: a violent hatred of Dr. Darcy himself. Shivering, James jumped to his feet and strode to his desk. Checking his Rolodex, he quickly phoned Darcy's office number.

Tom sighed as he reached for the phone across his desk and across the untouched ham sandwich that sat atop the most recent of his professional journals. He was very tired and he knew it.

"Dr. Darcy speaking," he said in his low, professionally neutral voice.

"Doctor? Fleming here. I thought I'd be getting your secretary," said James honestly. "Sorry to disturb you."

"Not at all. The secretary is out at the moment, and I'm not with a client."

James heard the uncharacteristic tiredness in Darcy's voice and was alerted.

"Listen, Darcy, I'd like to drop by and have a chat." James had suddenly changed his tune. He'd wanted a quick word with Darcy on the phone if possible, but now he wanted it in person.

"I've had a cancellation of my four o'clock appointment today."

James checked the daily calendar that lay on his desk, a duplicate of the one on Maggie's. A day of paperwork and a few phone calls stared back at him: his recent sedentary life flashed before him.

"Great, I'll be there. Just off the Dundrum road, yes?"

Darcy confirmed the street address and then paused.

"James, I'm glad you're coming. There are a couple of things I'd like to tell you about."

His curiosity pricked, James willed the rest of his dull afternoon away. Although Maggie's treat of a lamb kebab and a selection of cream cakes lifted his spirits momentarily, he had to face the fact, yet again, that his lucrative life as a lawyer specializing in property conveyancing often lacked enough interest to get him through the day.

As he drove out of the center of Dublin at three-thirty his thoughts drifted inevitably to Geraldine. And now he was fuming. It was one thing for Sarah to give him an ultimatum as she flew off to the States, literally out of sight and often out of mind. But Geraldine! She was another story. She was here, a matter of a few miles away from him, day after day. This arrogance was a new side to her. He leaned on his horn as the BMW slowed in front of him to make an illegal turn. His foot hovered over the accelerator of his beloved Citröen. He wished Darcy worked farther out of town; he wanted to let the Citröen roar through the countryside, on the flat roads of Kildare perhaps. As it was, he crawled through Windy Arbour, his thoughts engaged in an imaginary quarrel with Geraldine.

Agreeing with Sarah, no less. This was rich! They had never met, nor would they if he could help it. To hell with the both of them, he said aloud, but without any real force behind it. He pulled into a vacant space in the car park near Darcy's building and switched off the engine. And then what? he mused, deflated. Start again? Be alone, again?

James walked slowly toward the front entrance of the office building, noting its wheelchair accessible ramp, noting the brass plaques of the other medical personages who also had offices there. One day that could be Geraldine, he thought proudly. And speculating on the rental of such a desirable location, he thought immediately of his brother, Donald, holding forth in his own cozy surgery that had been built onto their mother's house. No doubt at their mother's expense! He wrenched his jealous thoughts away from his brother and his irritating ways and turned back to the matter at hand.

Quietly, he let himself into Darcy's simple waiting room. A tasteful mix of magazines lay waiting on the small mahogany end tables that bracketed the two-seated sofa. Two upholstered armchairs stood ready. Two heavy glass ashtrays stood empty on each table, and a discreet CD player-cum-radio was in one corner. Classical music—Beethoven, James thought—was playing softly. In another corner, on the floor, was a small, round white canister. It was plugged into a wall socket and James, puzzled at first, realized its hum filled the room with white noise, drowning out any voices that might carry through the closed door, which bore the narrow brass plaque with the name of Thomas Darcy. No initials, James noted, liking that.

These observations took only seconds, and at the clicking sound of the heavy outer door closing, the inner door silently opened and Tom Darcy strode out.

"James!" he said heartily, grasping James's extended hand.

"Dr. Darcy," said James, beaming in spite of himself.

"No, I told you, it's Tom," said the older man, indicating that James precede him into his office. The inner sanctum, thought James, trying to take things in at a glance.

"Sit, sit," said Tom, throwing himself into the leather chair that stood at his desk. James sat in the only other chair in the room, a match to the two in the waiting room.

"This is the patient's chair, I take it?" James was suddenly self-conscious.

"I refer to them as clients," said Tom easily. He

loosened his tie. James found himself loosening his own.

"Why is that?"

"I believe it helps the person to get away from the medical model. The word 'patient' has connotations, as you know, of physical illness. A patient comes to a medical situation already vulnerable, with a host of emotional and experiential baggage."

James, who had rarely had to seek a physician's help, looked at Tom questioningly.

"You see, James, when a patient is sick, he or she is frightened of things that are beyond the patient's control. The doctor still has a mystique. He's all-powerful, all-knowing, as a result, godlike. He has secret knowledge, or arcane knowledge . . ."

James scoffed.

"It's true, James. At a deep level, that is the patient's perception of the medical profession. But I am aware such attitudes are changing, for example, in the United States, because of many factors. The point is, the public, in other words, the patient, still lacks specialized knowledge—of drugs, or medical procedures and so on—and that lack of knowledge makes them feel helpless. Helplessness makes them feel trusting towards the doctor, but perhaps, underneath, it carries a hint of resentment?"

"Hardly," said James.

"I am talking about at a deep psychological level the patient isn't even aware of. Many patients tend to look upon their physicians as surrogate parents, and endow the physicians with a parent's authority. They regress emotionally, doing what they are told without questioning. Wanting to be good so that surrogate parent will take care of them, make them feel better. It's the dependency, you see, that they experience towards the physician. Now, in my line of work, I don't want to encourage dependency. Trust, certainly, but not a sense of powerlessness. Nor do I encourage the idea that I have all the answers."

"Surely you want the patient to do what you tell him?"

"No, no. I want the client to do what he thinks he should do in a given situation. We work together until he can find out what he feels and thinks. Together we try to find out patterns in his or her life, or events that influenced behaviors. We keep working until he can find the health and strength to act in a way that will help him. Mental illness is a disease of the spirit."

"But surely—"

"Oh yes, there are seriously ill people, and they may and do require hospital stays, or extensive drug treatments, perhaps even electroconvulsive therapy. As a physician I also treat them. As a physician I can treat the body as well as the mind, or the mind through the body. We know so much more now than we did. What was once thought of as possession by the devil, for hundreds of years, we now know with hindsight to have been schizophrenia. The breakthrough has been, with so many diagnoses, that the origin of the disease has a chemical basis, that the biochemistry of the brain can cause what was once thought to be characterological disturbances. I can diagnose and treat these illnesses, or refer them to other physicians, but over the years, as I worked in the field, I realized I was drawn more and more to psychotherapy—"

"The talking cure?"

"If you like. Essentially that is how it works."

Tom sensed James's incredulity from his skeptical expression.

"Think of it this way. Adults who have problems in their early twenties and onwards usually have had something lacking in their childhood. It could date from early childhood, even infancy. The factor that was lacking can range from something as essential to the child's emotional and physical survival as food or physical affection and contact to something relatively milder, such as a parent's approval. Thus there is a spectrum of quite serious problems, taking perhaps some years to ameliorate, which would involve long-term therapy, to other problems that take perhaps ten weeks or so to deal with, so-called short-term therapy."

"And this therapy will work because you talk and discuss things with the patient, pardon me, the client?" Tom watched as James began to shift in his seat, his fine long fingers tapping on the arms of his chair.

"Ah, not quite. The client comes to the therapist because he is in psychological distress; depression or anxieties are common reasons the person seeks help. Perhaps he is not achieving in his work or career, or he cannot maintain a lasting relationship with a woman. We begin there, with what is called the presenting problem. An analogy of an onion is often used. The person presents a problem or an issue and as we begin to address that initial problem as the client describes it, a first layer is peeled away, usually revealing another layer, and then another, and so on."

James nodded. "It's not that I need to be convinced, Tom, but . . ."

Tom waited.

James again moved uneasily in his chair.

Tom waited.

James spoke at last, under pressure of the silence. "It just strikes me that, well, why sit and bemoan one's fate? Why not just get on with it?"

"That is a characteristically Irish point of view, and rightly so," said Tom, watching James react to this statement.

"Oh, I see. The Irish are repressed." James's tone was bordering on sarcasm. "All our problems today are because of the oppression of the Catholic Church. I don't buy that!"

"Good, because that isn't what I am saying, James. I am not stereotyping; there are reasons for what I say. We just accept, for example, that the peoples who live around the Mediterranean are more open, more flamboyant perhaps, are more comfortable expressing themselves in words and conversation, in music and dance. Sometimes don't we envy them that temperament? Don't many of us flee there for sun holidays? It's not just the sunshine we crave, but the relaxed lifestyle.

"Do we stop to consider that those peoples

have lived for hundreds of years in a temperate climate, that physical life has been easier because of that. No damp winters or cold, bitter winds. The very fundamental tasks of life, which historically are agricultural, were physically easier, and that gave them more leisure time. Their food is wonderfully healthy, with abundant fruit and vegetables growing easily. Look at the climatic conditions: their days are longer than ours, even in winter. We have long summer nights here of course in the northern latitudes. But we have correspondingly shorter days in the winter. Imagine generations of Irish people toiling on the land—and the sun beginning to set at half three in the afternoon! Generations living in the long dark autumns and winters until the advent of electricity. In the last few hundred years, the weather in Ireland has been increasingly damp—"

"And it still is," laughed James ruefully. "But are you saying that short days and eternal dampness have made the Irish people repressed? Come now."

"Not as directly as that perhaps, but in a way. And remember, it was you who used the word repressed, not I. The Irish are an introspective bunch, but they then do not share those insights with one another. There has always been great value set on coping with the hardships of life, and not complaining. There is such a thing, is there not, of the Irish putting a brave face on things?"

James nodded.

"I know you've observed this. The Irish historically don't talk about their problems, and they certainly don't complain. They get on with it, as you say. They make the best of things."

"Wait a minute, Tom," James interrupted, "you know the Irish are considered to be great talkers—and perhaps as a consequence, great writers!"

"Oh, definitely. But they are not talking about themselves in any intimate way. They are wonderful, marvelous storytellers, from the dawn of the culture this has been their great gift, but the oral tales are about other people. In more modern times, the storyteller may tell a story against himself but the humor is always there to keep the distance between what is public and what is private. The wit of the Irish is based in irony, and as you know, irony is hard to penetrate. The writers you mention pour out their stories and insights onto paper—putting them at yet one remove from their audience. Irish authors have never been confessional! And then consider, some of our greatest writers left Ireland to free themselves, in complex ways. Joyce, Beckett, Yeats on and off throughout his life."

James nodded, reluctantly agreeing with Tom's observation.

"You agree that the Irish are stoical?" Tom waited.

"Yes, of course."

"And you should know that historically they did not seek medical help. Why? Perhaps because for generations there was none. And then when there was, the patient often couldn't be helped. Perhaps pain could be eased, but cures weren't available. Cancer, tuberculosis, arthritis. No help for these. There was a mentality of acceptance. Perhaps that attitude of acceptance was encouraged by that brand of Christianity that teaches endurance, patience, and a reward in the afterlife. To my mind the Irish accept things, and then proceed to endure them. And then, perhaps unlike other groups with similar histories, they keep their feelings to themselves."

"That's not a bad thing, surely!"

"In terms of surviving hundreds of years of oppression, of hardship, of famine, and remaining a cohesive people, no, it was not a bad thing. But those days are gone, and it is taking the nation, the people, the very individual, time to realize that—time, in a real sense, to catch up."

"And relax?"

"In a sense, yes. Life itself is becoming, has become, easier physically. Those great survival qualities of endurance and stoicism can loosen a little. And with that perhaps the great Irish interdiction against complaining, against talking about oneself. Don't you see that talking about oneself has been perceived—forever, if you ask me"—Tom smiled a wry smile—"as being weak. But it's all right to talk; it's good to talk. It can be a healthful thing. Surely you've seen the beginnings of change in our society as various individuals and organizations are starting to talk openly at last?"

James nodded sadly. Surely scandals had been almost daily rocking the nation: incest, child abuse, spousal abuse, financial intrigue, political corruption.

"We can't go back," Tom said as though reading James's mind.

James jumped, startled.

"Sorry," said Tom. "Comes with the territory."

"Yes, but . . . but for the ordinary person to sit here . . ."

"Yes, all my patients are ordinary individuals," said Tom seriously. "But terrible things happen to ordinary people. The ones who come to therapy are trying to deal with those things. Others are trying to grow, to solve problems that have stood in their way of having a little happiness—of having healthy relationships with their families, their lovers, their spouses, their friends."

James shifted again in his chair; little flashes of his recent scenes with both Sarah and Geraldine crossed his inner eye.

"Would you like to give it a try?" Tom said suddenly.

"Yes," James blurted and then recovered himself. "I mean to say, ah, yes, I think so."

"This is a little unorthodox, but I would like to work with you, James," Tom said seriously.

"Right, why, thank you." James was moved and confused. Slightly embarrassed at his too quick response, he regained his professional composure. "I'd like to think about it," he said at last. "But right now I'd like to get back to the case in hand."

Nodding, Tom stood up and retrieved a manila

folder from the filing cabinet. Opening it, James began to read through a small sheaf of papers. On each sheet was a short message, the words cut from newspapers. James looked up questioningly at Tom.

"How long has this been going on?" he said sharply.

"A few months," said Tom.

"What? And you didn't tell me?"

"No, I didn't. I saved them of course, but more out of psychiatric interest than anything else. I don't believe there is a connection between these and Quixote."

"Have you received any of these since the horse's death?"

"No."

James read each message carefully. Each consisted of a single simple sentence:

Honor your father and mother.

Psychiatrists are sick.

You'll live to regret this.

You have no right.

Washing dirty linen.

Physician heal thyself.

James studied the envelopes first. They were blue, like the stationery, a familiar brand available in newsagents and shops throughout the country. All were posted at the general post office on O'Connell Street. The stamps were ordinary. Everything was common and without character. Darcy's name and address were printed, neatly but childishly, in blue ink. The messages, however, were made up of individual clipped letters. Their typefaces and size were similar, even familiar.

"Do you have any ideas?" James was still showing his annoyance with Tom.

"No, I don't. Obviously I deal with very unhappy people. There are times when they become very angry with me."

"How do you know that?"

"Well, some have the courage and enough health to actually tell me. Others begin to skip appointments or cease to come altogether. Some write me letters and then do not return. I am talking about twenty years of practice, James. I admit I have never received letters quite like these before, but when these first started, I wasn't alarmed. I'm still not."

"Do you have any idea who sent them?"

"No."

"But you are showing them to me now?"

"You asked if anything unusual had happened lately."

"Come on, Tom. Clearly this person is angry with you. Perhaps angry enough to kill your horse?"

"It's my turn to say 'oh come on,' James," said Tom, annoyed for the first time. "Look at the leap between the two acts. One, there is someone anonymously clipping out letters and pasting them on paper, secretly and like a child, perhaps a naughty child, or an angry child. That tells me this person is a loner or timid or someone who does not confront the people or the issues in his life—"

"You assume it's a man then?"

"Oh, why, yes," said Tom, hesitating. "Yes, without thinking I assumed it was a man. Let me see, my impression would be both from the tone of the sentences and the method, that it is a male, and not an adolescent. Someone very troubled. Hemmed in, perhaps. Very angry with the profession. Frustrated. Someone who is bottling up his emotions. My gut sense is a woman would be more direct, less circuitous. But I'd have to examine why I think that. It might be a bias of my own."

"Oh for God's sake Tom!" James exploded. Tom looked at him in genuine surprise.

"What?"

"Someone sends you threatening letters in a queer anonymous way, and you stand here analyzing them—no, not them, yourself!"

Tom looked startled.

"You said it was a leap between an act like this, these letters, and killing a horse. Why?"

"Simply put, one is fairly passive and the other is active."

"I don't agree. Tell me, you think it was a man but you're not sure."

"Okay," Tom replied reluctantly.

"Couldn't a woman have killed Quixote as easily—no, not easily, but as readily as a man?"

"Actually yes. In fact that was one thing I wanted to tell you . . . Mrs. Killian rang me earlier. She got the results of the necropsy. She related the results to me. The major artery in Quixote's throat was severed and she bled to death very quickly. Anyone who was determined could have looked this up in a book of animal husbandry, a veterinarian textbook. It wouldn't have taken great strength, it would have taken knowledge, a large, very sharp knife . . ." Tom shuddered as he forced out the words. "And . . ."

"And?" said James feeling cold himself.

"And, in my opinion, someone with iron nerve."

They sat in silence for a few minutes as James absorbed this news.

"Not to press my point too hard, Tom, but clearly the killer of the horse could be a man or a woman, the sender of these letters likewise. They could be the same person. I want you to think about any of your patients who could be this angry with you. The letters stopped once Quixote was dead—there's an obvious link."

"What do you mean?"

"That this person has escalated his or her actions against you. Think. Do you have any gut reaction?"

"Again, no." Tom's tone was more defensive now. "None of my patients would do this. I've had scores of patients. If it is someone really disturbed it could be someone another therapist dealt with . . ."

James stood up, exasperated.

"Look, James, I am not alarmed by these letters."

"Oh, but you should be, Tom. These, taken with the death of the horse, paint a very different picture than either of the events taken separately. You seem to be fighting me on this. You know,

Tom, I have some expertise of my own in criminal matters."

Tom recognized James's pique and his own stubbornness. "Okay." Tom sighed. "I take your point." He paused. "Then I ought to tell you the rest."

"There's more!" James was animated.

"Again, I have taken these things as random events. Well, for what it's worth, come with me."

Tom, carefully locking doors on his way, led James to the car park. Wordlessly, he pointed to a number of scorings on the paint of his car. Some seemed small random scratches or gouges, but one on the driver's side door seemed to be a crude drawing of an eye, an open eye.

Tom and James agreed that it could be an eye; the scratches seemed less random. James made as accurate a sketch of the drawing as he could and indicated he would be back in the near future with a camera. Meanwhile he managed to get Tom to agree that he could bring the letters to the police for possible analysis.

James was silent then as they walked back to the office, Tom unlocking doors along the way. He was relieved to see Tom's habitual caution.

They were still standing in Tom's office. Tom seemed restless and James sensed a change in his mood.

"Clearly this is serious, Tom."

Tom nodded, fingering the few items on his Spartan desk.

"I suppose it looks like that, doesn't it?"

"To tell you the truth, I would consider any

one of these to be serious on its own, but given the time frame I think they have to be linked. Tell me, have you had to endure this kind of thing over the years?"

"No, the most I would get were telephone calls. People who object to my work, who don't believe in it. They'd use up valuable time on my tape. But the bulk of the taped calls I used to get were just clients who needed to hear my voice . . ."

"Your voice?" James exclaimed.

"Oh yes, if the therapist has become the anchor for the person undergoing a crisis, just the sound of my voice can be reassuring." Tom smiled in a self-deprecating way.

"God," James murmured half aloud, struck by this picture of archetypal loneliness. He'd been to the fringes of that abyss, but had never gone over. He looked at Tom with new eyes.

"Look, Tom. Think hard, is there anything else you can tell me? Any suspicions?"

"It's very difficult for me to think in these terms, James." Tom sat heavily in his chair, his face a little grayer than before.

"You must imagine to yourself what my work is like. Sometimes, depending on the client and the problem, I am mother or father, sibling or husband. I am a mirror to them—so that they can see themselves in me. Or I am a screen, neutral, and not a reflection. Often, I am at least in the sessions a role model of psychological health. The therapist too"—Tom smiled briefly—"has to work hard to maintain his own health and balance. A therapist can't live with suspicion. I can accept that my clients or patients, the very ill ones, have destructive or violent tendencies and work with them on those. But I can't always be looking over my shoulder. I must avoid such paranoid-like behavior. So, to answer your question, no, I don't have any suspicions, because I can't afford to. I would seize up, I would lose my effectiveness."

"Still, try to answer my question," James prodded him.

Tom sighed. Reluctantly he finally admitted to James that he had a sense that someone was following him. But he had struggled to get this fearfulness under control.

"Then you do sometimes feel afraid?"

"No, not in the sense you mean. James, I don't fear that someone will jump out of the bushes and attack me. I am more fearful that I am losing at times my center, that something in my own life is being projected."

James looked blank.

"Simply put, I must fight my imagination. If something is wrong in my personal life or my professional life, or with my attitude towards my patients, then perhaps it is taking the form of a sense of insecurity, vulnerability. Worse, a sense that someone is watching me . . ."

James threw his hands in the air. "Tom," he said explosively, startling them both. "Look, this is real. Threatening letters, damage to your car, a sense you are being followed or watched, and the vicious killing of your horse, *your* horse, not the stable's horse."

He slapped his hands on the table and leaned over it, stopping himself as he saw Tom subtly push his chair back from the desk.

"Sorry, Tom, sorry," he said quickly, standing up, pulling back.

Tom merely looked at him quizzically.

"Sorry," James said again. "I just wanted to make you see that you may well be in some danger, real physical danger—not some metaphysical, some existential danger of losing your center, for chrissakes!"

"That's all right, James. I can see your concern."

"I want you to ring me if there is anything out of the ordinary, anything at all, no matter how small. You are not objective."

Tom laughed silently.

James smiled in return, the tension between them evaporating. "Let me be the judge here, Tom. Your point of view is difficult for me to accept, or even to understand, but I do accept it. It is your way. Let me handle this part of your life at least."

Tom raised his eyebrows at this last remark, but James failed to notice. He prepared to take his leave, realizing that an hour had sped past.

Tom stood and walked him to the door. "I appreciate this, James. You have my word, I'll let you know if there is anything else."

"Good, good." James's voice was firm, parental.

The two men shook hands warmly.

Tom called after him as James walked away.

"If you incur any expenses I will—"

But James's upraised hand silenced him.

* * *

As James pulled out of the car park he made a quick decision and turned south. Pulling into a nearby shopping center he quickly called into a newsagent's, and using their machine, made a number of Xerox copies of the letters and of his own sketch of the crude eye scratched on Tom's car door. With copies in hand, he arrived at the garda station in Stepaside and asked to speak to the officer, Crowley by name, who was in charge of the Darcy investigation. Carefully holding the letters in gloved hands, Crowley read them slowly and with consideration. At length he agreed with James that they should be sent to the Dublin forensic office for a complete analysis—fingerprints, paper, glue, the lot. Dr. Darcy himself would be fingerprinted, for purposes of elimination.

It was a long shot, they both agreed, but worth pursuing.

"How well do you know this Darcy?" Crowley asked as he walked James toward the front door.

"Well enough. Why do you ask?" James smiled, for he liked the man. "You sound a little wary of him."

"Oh, it's his being a psychiatrist. You know, the general feeling. Maybe he's a bit unstable himself?"

Crowley let the question hang.

"Are you suggesting he killed the horse himself?" James laughed out loud.

"It wouldn't be for the insurance. We've checked that. No, I'm not really suggesting he did this himself. Or the letters either. But he must be

dealing with some unstable people, am I right."
It was a statement.

"Well, if it's a patient, you've got a problem.
He's a medical doctor, as I'm sure you know. He's
not going to reveal anything about his patients."

"Nonetheless, I'll be having a chat with him
when he comes in for the fingerprinting."

James had felt relieved that he'd taken some
action on Darcy's behalf, but admitted to himself
that it surely wasn't enough. Crowley's comments
reinforced his own unease about Darcy's situation and his seeming lack of caution for himself.
Stuck at a long traffic light coming into
Ranelagh, he impulsively picked up his cell
phone and punched in Darcy's number.

"Thomas Darcy."

James felt a surge of relief.

"Tom, James here. Listen, I was just thinking."
James hesitated, amazed at what he heard himself saying. "I'd like to take you up on that offer,
if it still stands."

"Yes," Tom's voice was neutral and James felt a
quick pang of annoyance with the man.

"About the—"

"Yes, I know. When would it be convenient for
you, days or evenings?"

"Oh." James was again at a loss. "Evenings, I
imagine," he said quickly as the line of traffic
began to move and he needed to shift gears.
"Evenings."

"Right, let me see." There was a pause. "Look,
I have an hour free at the end of my day tomorrow, at five. Why not come by then for an initial

session? If you find that you would like to continue, we can, in due course, fix a regular day and time that suits us both."

"Right. See you then," James said slowly.

What have I done now? thought James, as surprise at his own impulsiveness struck him. What have I done indeed?

CHAPTER

—— 11 ——

As JAMES ENTERED the office, he noted immediately that Tom's manner was more professional. Disturbingly to James's mind, Darcy seemed more formal and distant. James sat in the chair he had so recently sat in, but realized that he was now on very different ground.

"Right, James. What I am going to go over with you now are a series of agreements between us; these are called the ground rules of therapy. Ordinarily we would agree to a day and time at this point, but because of our scheduling situation, as I said, we can deal with that part later. In the event that we decide to work together, I will keep a specific time free for you, every week, and I will tell you sufficiently in advance if I am going on vacation or to a conference. You likewise will let me know if you cannot keep your appointment. If you do not give me sufficient advance notice, then you will be billed for that missed session because clearly I must keep it always available for you. You should know that I keep fifty-minute hours. The reason for that is ..." James realized Darcy had noticed his smirk, "it gives the therapist time to make notes, review the session, reflect on what's been said, before the next client arrives.

"Secondly, we will agree on a fee. My standard hourly rate is ..." and here he mentioned a figure that seemed high to James, especially since his own insurance didn't cover such mental health matters; however, he willingly nodded his agreement.

"Third, you will agree to tell me whatever comes into your mind during our session together. In therapy the client knows that he has the full time and attention of the therapist, but sometimes the hour will hang heavy. There are reasons that you will feel this way, which will become apparent as we work through your issues. At other times, your hour will seem too brief. But you will use your time here well, telling me what concerns you, and I in turn will try to help you understand. This is insight-oriented therapy and together we will work towards an understanding of behavior, of patterns old and new."

Tom was quiet then and James looked at him expectantly.

"Yes?" he said questioningly.

"Go on."

"Go on? I haven't even started. What am I supposed to do?"

"All right." Tom smiled encouragingly. "Why

don't you start by telling me a little about yourself. Your family situation. Are you married?"

James laughed and suddenly stopped. He wondered why he had laughed. "No, I'm not married," he said quickly. Laughing again, James realized he was nervous. "But not for want of trying." He smiled and then was self-conscious that he had smiled and so smiled again in an embarrassed way.

"You've been involved, ah, committed, but it didn't lead to marriage?" Tom looked at James seriously, having ignored the nervous laughter, and James realized he was attempting to help him get started, much as he himself would assist one of his clients who was reticent or uneasy.

"I wasn't actually engaged, no, but I thought the relationship would lead in that direction. I suppose I thought in some vague way that we'd end up married. I was young, God, quite young now, looking back." James paused, remembering. Suddenly he could see himself in his mind's eye—so young, in his twenties, a formless, gormless youth!

"Her name was Teresa. Oh, it's a long time ago. Ancient history."

Tom remained silent, but somehow the silence wasn't empty, and James felt pressured to keep talking.

"It was a college romance. She has three children now."

Again he paused.

"I had, you see, I have this passion for steam trains. It's my hobby—the way other men play golf or ride horses or travel. I do all that, of

course, but since I was a boy I have had a fasci-
nation with trains, the actual physical train
engines in particular. I had toy trains, I read
about trains, I traveled in order to ride on trains.
At the end of my years at Trinity I had an opportunity to go on a trip to Russia, on the Transibe-
rian railway. And this was long before glasnost! I
had asked Teresa to go with me but she wasn't
interested. Then she agreed halfheartedly. And
then, well, the week we were to leave she told me
her true feelings. She really hadn't wanted to go."

James paused again. How headstrong he
seemed now. He recalled that her parents hadn't
wanted her to go. Why would they? His own
mother hadn't been too keen—the impropriety of
it all.

Thoughts and memories, and faint, ghostlike
images seen at a great distance, muted and soft,
passed through his mind at the speed of light.

With altered mood he looked up at Tom's face.

"Now that I think about it, I suppose I was a bit
arrogant about it all. I just laughed and said the
time would fly by. I suppose I was selfish or
maybe thoughtless ... actually it was a brilliant
trip ... the biggest train experience I'd had until I
went to Peru. Anyway, we didn't correspond—I
think I sent her a few postcards." He paused
again. "I see now that I had taken her for granted,
assumed she'd always be waiting there for me,
even though we had no understanding." James
paused again, caught up in a more mature version
of what he was now seeing in hindsight. He was
reminded suddenly of Geraldine, even of Sarah.

"When I got back to Dublin I was as high as a kite with the adventures I'd had and the sights I'd seen. I rang Teresa straight away and she told me bluntly she'd met someone else and was engaged to be married."

James was silent for a long time.

"How did this affect you, James?"

"Oh, I got over it."

"Did you?"

"Of course, that was years ago."

Tom was silent again, and again James felt a pressure to continue.

"Yes, I got over her," he said after a pause. "Actually since you've asked, I didn't. I used to think about her, I would feel angry that she'd not waited. I resented that I couldn't have my great train trip without paying this great cost when I got back. I mourned about her for a long time. But now that we're talking about it I'm wondering perhaps if I was moping around because she dumped me, and not because I loved her. Perhaps it was wounded pride and not a great loss?" James stopped suddenly.

"Go on," said Tom.

"Perhaps it was meant to be," James said at last.

"Meant to be? That's a bit Irish, isn't it? A way of saying aloud one accepts what couldn't have been altered? Let's look at it from a different point of view, shall we. You and Teresa had a long college romance, an exclusive one. Perhaps you both needed a break, but each in your own way was unwilling either to acknowledge that to yourselves or each other. The trip gave you a built-in reason to have a fairly lengthy break, three months was a long time. You left with no stated commitment between you. Teresa took advantage, in the healthy sense of that word, of being free, without what perhaps had become a comfortable habit of having you around. She was free to meet someone at a point in her life when she was more mature, a graduate, starting a career. You on the other hand were also free. You weren't looking to meet someone, but you were looking for the freedom and adventure that new horizons hold. You too had reached a turning point, graduating from university and taking a break before you started your law career.

"James," Tom continued, "it may well have suited you both to have those three months apart in order to find out who you were and what you wanted. And it would seem that you didn't want each other."

James sat, trying to absorb this. The inner truth he hadn't wanted to acknowledge and the old habit of feeling sorry for himself fought each other with the power of entrenched beliefs.

"Well," he continued, his voice a little colder, "after that I dated lots of girls, but none seriously until I met Sarah, and I didn't meet her in the ordinary sense, not the way that most people intend that to mean."

"Then what do you mean?"

"I was much older when I met Sarah—during the course of a private case I had become involved in."

Tom listened attentively as James struggled to convey the complicated story of the Moore sisters, Violet, Lily, and poor Rose, of their dairy farm and the violent death of Jack Moore. He spoke of his significant role in tracking down the killer of Jack Moore. Finally he spoke of how in the thick of things Sarah had become very important to him. He told Tom proudly of her world renown as a violinist.

"What are you thinking?" Tom prompted, as James was silent for a long time.

"I'm remembering a special day we had, at the house we'd bought. It had extensive grounds, well it still has, and we'd, well, we'd made love on the grass in a dell not far from the house. We were walking back and my mother . . ."

"Go on."

"My mother arrived bearing lilacs, as usual. She bears lilacs when she visits . . ."

"As a courtesy?" Tom hid a smile.

"No, no, a ritual, I think. Or a shield, she holds them in front of her as though they are an introduction or a so-called viable excuse." Annoyance crept into his voice.

"It was the last truly happy time I had with Sarah. After that she went on tour. Oh, I'm happy for her success of course. And I worked on the house, our house, for a long time, getting it ready in a way. And Mother would pop down, always Mother. She was always 'popping down.'" James's voice had an adolescent ring to it.

"James, where do you call home?" Tom asked, seemingly abruptly.

"I, well, not that house."

"Yes."

James shrugged. "My flat, I guess, but . . ."

"But what?"

"Right now it just seems like a place to sleep."

"Any where else then?"

"Well, not my mother's house," James said angrily.

"No home then?"

"That's ridiculous, that's like saying a stockbroker owned no stock. I am a lawyer. I own property. I have an interest in a small hotel in Sligo where my ward lives. She's getting to be quite a young woman and managing very well." James briefly related the circumstances of the case, which had brought him so much pain and joy.

"Thank you for telling me that," said Tom.

James was surprised at what he perceived to be unexpected praise, and he felt irrationally proud of himself when Tom said it.

"You know, I don't talk about personal things to people," James heard himself say, as if to explain something.

"No one?" Tom said softly.

"Ah . . ." James hesitated. "I did. I used to talk to Matt. We were in school together, and then at university. He's in Australia now with his wife and children—oh, not forever," James added hastily. "He's on a sabbatical, teaching out there. I was pleased for him and the family, the kids will love it, such an experience!"

"And you miss him?"

James felt the color rise to his usually pale face.

"Seems that way." James moved quickly off that subject. "I find lately that I've been able to confide in Geraldine a bit, but not about Sarah, of course."

"Geraldine?"

"Oh." James realized that Tom didn't know everything about him, although at that moment he was feeling that in some, perhaps mystical, way that he did.

"Geraldine is another woman I am seeing." He tried to convey to Tom how he'd also met Geraldine through another case he'd solved; that she was a physician, almost fully qualified; that she'd grown up in the country and was full of fun and fire; that she had a great style of her own. Her hair, her eyes, her lips . . . James became self-conscious and again he stopped.

"She's lively, she's bright, she's very sexy, too. I am proud of her, she's doing very well."

"Hmmm," Tom said by way of an answer.

James's attention drifted off. He looked at the framed watercolor of irises and peonies on the wall behind Tom's head, staring at it as so many patients had before him, feeling a little tired, but strangely relaxed.

"That painting, you know, the combination of flowers is unlikely, but nonetheless it works. It's very, I don't know, evocative."

"In what way?" said Tom, leaning forward.

"I suppose it's the colors, but I'm not sure. I'm not very good at art either. Music, books are more to my liking. Those are my mother's interests too. But Dad now, he liked to paint a little in his spare time."

James looked up quite suddenly, at a loss, surprised by the catch in his voice.

"Tell me about that," said Tom.

James felt suddenly resentful and shook his head stubbornly.

"Go on, try," whispered Tom.

"Dad is dead."

"I'm sorry." Tom paused. "Can you talk about him a bit? I think the picture reminded you of something."

"He liked to do watercolors, not as good as that of course, but not bad either. I think he did it more as a hobby. After he washed the car in the driveway on Saturday, he'd have his dinner with Mother and me and Donald. And then, if it were a fine day, he'd pack his easel, and his wooden box with the paints, and a bottle of water for the brushes. He'd make a flask of tea in the kitchen and then he'd take out the special paper he used for his paintings. He kept it in a special portfolio by the dresser in his bedroom. He'd load it all into the Rover and off he'd go. Off to Wicklow Town, or up to the Feather Bed, or the Dublin mountains." James heaved an enormous sigh, his eyes suddenly filling with tears that he tried to hide.

"What are you feeling now?" Tom said very softly.

"Oh." James seemed to breathe out from the bottom of his lungs. "As though I were nine or so. I can see him in my mind's eye . . ."

"And yourself?"

"Yes, standing in the drive, watching him go off. I was always happy for him."

"Why?"

"Oh, he seemed to be getting away, he seemed to be free, if only for that short Saturday afternoon. He'd come back with a wind-red face and a smile. He'd take out his pipe when he saw me and he'd ruffle my hair."

"And you? You seemed moved just now, flooded with feelings."

"I don't know. That's a funny question." He looked at Tom, who merely raised his eyebrows.

"All right, all right," said James, annoyed suddenly. "I was happy for him, but I was sad he was leaving. I suppose you could say I wanted to go with him."

"You said just now that he was free."

"That's just an expression." James straightened in his chair, irritable and confused. "I don't quite see where this is going, Tom," he said crossly.

"What was he free of, on those Saturdays you describe, hmmm . . . ?"

"Oh, I don't know, me perhaps?" James looked up at Tom.

"You?"

"I guess I felt excluded, all right? And then there was Mother, he was free of Mother." James again felt the confusion, a sense of alarm, of too much revealed. He shifted in his chair yet again and shook his head, signaling he would say no more. There was silence and he felt it as a tension between himself and Tom. He glanced at Tom and away.

"Well, now, let me see," Tom said by way of an answer as he slid his tie between his index and middle finger in an habitual gesture. He seemed lost in thought, but only for a few seconds, whereupon he looked at James directly.

"You've worked very hard, James, for your first session. I am very pleased with that. And you've . . ."

James beamed suddenly at this praise and relaxed.

"You've touched on many issues. But the theme I am hearing today is a sense of loss. You've spoken now of two men, very important in your emotional life, who are gone from you. Your father, who is dead, and your friend Matt, who is at quite a distance in Australia. And you've also spoken of the significant women in your life, Teresa of course, who in a sense left you when you took a stand about something important to you, but who also perhaps mirrored what you were feeling yourself at the time: a need to separate, to find space, to meet other people. Nonetheless, she was a loss you were unprepared for. Then there is Sarah, who seems to be present in your life, but who, as you've told me, is also gone, physically gone away to the United States. You are feeling these losses and they affect you at many levels. And then there is Geraldine, who although she is here, is threatening to leave you if you do not do things the way she has indicated. You've also indirectly mentioned your mother and you know as well as I there is some anger there, and a distance. You were not only excluded from your father's pastimes, but from your mother's emotional life, and you felt that keenly. Perhaps you still do, but that's perhaps for another day."

James felt himself stiffen in self-consciousness.

Tom continued, talking about what he saw as James's sense of rejection, the sense of estrangement he seemed to feel from his own family, possibly from early on in his childhood.

James found himself wordlessly but definitely shaking his head in disagreement.

Tom continued, very gently half smiling at James's obvious defiance. "I think we might work on your sense of abandonment, for that is what it is called, in our next session. Another area we might consider is this dichotomy you describe between Sarah and Geraldine.

"On the one hand there is Sarah, a woman who seems, from your description, to be emotionally remote, from you at least, and perhaps it is her general mien, I can't say. But what I see in my imagination is an odalisque. She is on a pedestal and you, James, are keeping her there. You will have to look at why.

"Then there is Geraldine, who is, in your own words, a woman of vitality, clearly a very giving, caring person, vibrant. Life-affirming. A hands-on physician. Someone who might even be fun?" Tom smiled, looking at James quizzically, lightening the sting of his words. The acute embarrassment James was feeling was showing on his face.

"All right," said Tom when he got no response. "You seem to have set up an opposition between two rather emblematic types of women. And you are classically in the middle. I suggest that you reflect a little on why you are drawn to two such women and what it is that may be keeping you at a distance from both of them. Now, our time is up."

"Oh!" James said, surprised and disappointed and relieved all in the one thought. He asked for a second appointment and between them they arranged a time for Thursday lunchtime.

As James continued to sit there not knowing what to do, Tom stood up slowly and walked to the door.

"Until next time, James."

James, feeling slightly dazed, drove slowly back to town. Finding the idea of "going home" suddenly laden with emotional baggage, he left his car at his flat and walked to his local pub, where he had a quiet drink by himself. He hadn't liked that word "abandonment" and in order to ease his mind, resolved he would explain to Tom next week that he certainly had absolutely no sense of being abandoned. On finishing his second pint, he admitted to himself that he'd actually liked talking to Tom, and with a rush of affection he ordered a third pint in order to enjoy his sense of relaxation that was brought on by being understood by another person.

On his return to his spacious flat, James spread the copies he had made of the letters and his own sketch of the eye on his large smoked glass dining table that blended so well with the monochrome theme of his decor. Pulling up one of the black leather chairs that rolled quietly on its chromium wheels, he sat down to study them afresh. The letters were so simple that he had already committed them to memory. Now he wanted to see them with new eyes, to let whatever thoughts he might have float into his mind.

First, he wondered, why were they so short? Perhaps because it was difficult for the person to cut them out. They could have been written— why weren't they? Does this person think Darcy would know his handwriting? He could print. Why not cut out entire words—why each separate letter of each word?

Why did Darcy assume it was a man? That was my first mistake too, thought James, standing up suddenly.

"I'm not objective here," he said aloud to the refrigerator as he opened the door and pulled out some roast beef, some sliced cheese, and a bottle of mustard. As he made a sandwich and put on some coffee to brew he shook his head to clear his thoughts and start again.

CHAPTER
—— 12 ——

MR. EDWARDS SEATED himself as he had done almost every Thursday for the past six months and looked gravely at Tom Darcy.

"Well, Dr. Darcy, as usual I don't know where to begin."

Tom waited for a minute or so, and when the silence continued, he prompted, "Just tell me the first thing that comes into your mind."

"All right," said Mr. Edwards in his very cultured, highly educated Dublin accent. "Work is going very well."

As Tom knew, Edwards was the executive director of a middle-sized manufacturing company that exported small medical devices, particularly to the United States. It was a thriving enterprise. He had joined the company at twenty-two and now, in his early forties, he not only ran the company with great expertise and foresight, but made an excellent living.

Tom suppressed a yawn as Edwards recounted the details of a recent meeting of the board of directors which dealt with choosing a charity to be recipient of some substantial funds.

"I imagine that is good for the corporate image of your company," said Tom, casually but with deliberate provocation.

Edwards looked at him with a sudden flash of anger.

"Well, isn't it?" Tom persisted.

"Yes, I suppose that's part of it."

"Then perhaps what you are really talking about is your own image. One of your concerns is the image you project . . . you really care what other people think of you."

"Doesn't everyone?" Edwards replied quickly.

Tom rather pointedly glanced at Edwards's fine leather shoes, at the expensive cuff links, the tie showing beneath the waistcoat.

"No, everyone is not concerned with his image in the same way. And when someone is, to the degree that it interferes with other things in his life, then it can be seen to be a problem."

"I don't like the way this is going, Doctor."

"You know, Mr. Edwards, we have to deal with the issue you raised last week. Think about it. You will see that you talk about the events of your week in a superficial way. Although those superficial yet realistic events of your life, as you present them, do inevitably reveal a theme. I want to help you move towards the real issues, the ones that drove you to seek help some months ago. And the one you touched on last time . . ."

"Darcy, you are insulting me when you call me superficial," Edwards observed.

"I don't think I insult you if I state my observations. When I said you were concerned with image, what I was reacting to was your staying with the surface of things." Tom was hoping he had soothed his client, but Edwards was defensive now, and Tom had put him there.

"Okay," Tom said gently. "Why don't we talk a little about your marriage."

"Such as it was." Edwards sounded bitter.

"Well, it was . . . exactly that."

"Short and unsuccessful. Have you forgotten? I am divorced. You know that. We both had to go abroad to do it since this benighted country didn't offer such a thing, even to Protestants like me—at that time."

"No, I haven't forgotten. But look, Mr. Edwards. You married. That is a serious act—a legal one, a contractual one, a social one. You went that far. You formed a relationship, and in marrying . . ."

"Judith."

"Excuse me?" Tom was startled.

"Her name was Judith, I told you that also." Mr. Edwards was visibly annoyed.

"I'm sorry. Okay, when you married Judith it was to form a lifetime union." Tom faltered. "And . . ."

"And?"

"Sorry, I was distracted. My thought is this: you had a relationship that led to marriage. Even though the marriage didn't last, nonetheless, you had one. That's not to be taken lightly."

There was a long silence. Tom waited. He'd wanted really to steer him back to the sexual issues that he now believed, with reason, that Edwards had. Tom knew that it was this deeper issue that was causing Edwards's inability to sleep. Even with the sleeping pills Tom had prescribed, Edwards recounted that his sleep was destroyed nightly by what he described as dreadful dreams.

"You suggested once that your marriage had not been consummated . . ."

"Yes."

"And . . ."

"Oh, God, if you must know, that was mutual."

"Neither of you was, let me see, neither of you was interested in the physical part of your marriage."

"No." Edwards was abrupt.

"Had you been interested when you were dating?"

"I don't know. It was a brief courtship. She was a spinsterish kind of woman, a longtime friend of the family on my father's side. She was Protestant. She was . . ."

Tom was silent

"She was always there. We had drinks, attended concerts, social events. I often need a, I suppose, a companion at such functions. This went on for years and somehow we became a couple. We were invited everywhere after a while as a couple. There were expectations . . . So I proposed. We had a very small wedding and a brief honeymoon in England. She fell sick, flu I think. Things drifted." He looked up at Tom. "Frankly I felt nothing for her. In due course we separated and divorced quietly. I never see her."

Tom was struck by the man's coldness. There was a long silence.

"Listen, Darcy, this strikes me as prurient interest on your part. I've told you—I don't want to discuss these matters."

Tom knew he couldn't pursue this line if the patient weren't willing.

"How are you sleeping?" he said, trying yet another tack.

Edwards spoke with more equanimity. "Well, I got about four hours last night, total. Between the waking up and the drifting off and the dozing."

"And you are still going to bed at the same time—"

"Dr. Darcy. I have religiously observed the regimen. No caffeine, no alcohol, no stimulation. I rise at the same time and retire at the same time. A fanatically Catholic monk could not be more abstemious than I."

"Exercise?" Tom remained firm in the face of Edwards's anger.

"But of course. I ride. You know that too."

Tom looked startled. Yes, he had known that but he'd blocked it. Why was he blocking so much today? he wondered, alarmed. He shifted his position. He was reminded of Quixote.

"Your own horse?"

"Yes, of course."

Tom kept his face a blank but inside he recognized a jealousy he hadn't felt in years. Jealousy

of this man—his class, his privilege, the years
with his own horse.

"I hunt. Old family friends have a place in
Wicklow. Actually I am rather glad the season is
almost on us."

"Season?"

"Hunting." Edwards was studying his fingernails. Groomed smooth hands, Tom observed.
Almost delicate yet large. He pictured Edwards
dressed for the hunt and anger surged through
him. He didn't like even the idea of hunting.

"But with this regimen you have me on, I ride
every morning before I go in to the office. Naturally my time is my own."

"Spicy food?" Tom needed to get away from
thinking about the horse.

"I beg your pardon?"

"Are you avoiding spicy food?"

"Yes."

Tom thought he said it with disdain.

"Okay, then let me suggest . . ." Tom sought for
the right words to encourage Edwards to relax his
guard, to trust him as he had, however briefly, at
their previous session. "Tell me if you can remember any dreams that you had last night, even during the week, no matter what the content."

Edwards glanced up from his nails, his face a
mask.

"I try not to remember them, as you know."

"Well, try now."

"All right. The bit I remember is totally out of
any kind of context. I'm walking along a busy
street. It is sunny and warm and the pedestrians

are bustling past me. I am in very good form. Wait . . . and I know, no, I don't have a destination, or else I don't remember now. A woman approached me, well dressed, middle-aged. Let me see, she was, you could see at a glance, a respectable, well-heeled person—from the clothes, the brooch, the deportment. Understand I knew all this in a split second, and just as I did, she slapped me across the face and said 'how dare you call me a fat old woman.' "

Edwards fell silent. Tom watched as he unconsciously stroked the side of his face.

"Do you have any associations with this dream?"

"None."

"And this woman was a stranger?"

"Totally. I didn't recognize her."

"Not familiar in any way?" Tom pressed him.

Edwards hesitated. "Well, perhaps, but only vaguely."

Tom nodded. There was a silence as Mr. Edwards grew restive. Tom had noticed how uncomfortable any silence made Mr. Edwards, and so consciously he used the silence to pressure Edwards to make deeper associations.

"Mr. Edwards, I think you know that the woman is your mother."

"You mustn't refer to that again," Edwards said sternly.

"I have to, Mr. Edwards. The trauma, the ordeal you suffered, is at the core of your distress now—"

"I regret ever confiding that in you. It is a

closed chapter. I do not wish to speak of it and I prefer that you don't speak of it."

Tom knew he risked driving this patient away from him, but he took the chance that he could educate the man in front of him, make him see that bringing out his feelings could help him.

"Mr. Edwards," he said kindly. "The mind doesn't work that way. Your mind won't allow that now. The dreams, the nightmares, are the memory forcing its way up to consciousness. Your mind wants you to deal with the issue, to confront it. Mr. Edwards, in doing so you will achieve rest in the deepest sense of the word. I want to help you to heal."

"I'm fine, I've already told you that."

"Well, then, let me talk about your dream. The woman is your mother—"

"Please."

Tom spoke in a level, measured tone, knowing that what he would say would agitate Mr. Edwards even further.

"The woman in the dream is your mother. Your description fits. In the dream she is the age she was when she seduced you. Her face is different in the dream—you don't know her as your mother because when she seduced you, you did not know her as your mother either. She approached you in a different form, a sexual, seductive form. In that seductive form she was a stranger to you." Tom watched as ugly red patches formed on Mr. Edwards's patrician face.

"I suspect that to you her body did appear old, perhaps she also was overweight, I don't know.

You do know, though. For a young boy, the body of an older woman will look its age. No longer firm, loose flesh on the thighs—" Tom stopped suddenly.

"Dr. Darcy, I will ask you to stop. Your interpretation is ludicrous, and I reject it. My mother is a distinguished, active woman. She has a certain place in society as we know it. I see my mother frequently—this is intolerable, I tell you!"

"No, Mr. Edwards. It is not in your best interests to be seeing your mother at this time. I suggest you tell her that. You need to be free of her immediate presence in order to work this issue through."

"That's ridiculous." Mr. Edwards's voice rose.

"Mr. Edwards. You have confided to me that she seduced you—you must let me help you. "

"Doctor, you have taken one sentence out of all the sentences I must have said here and blown it out of proportion. I say, that is enough!" Edwards was clearly in a rage.

Tom was about to add that then the nightmares would stop, but he could see that Mr. Edwards was closing down. He had shifted his body away from Tom. Tom's heart was racing. He knew he'd taken a chance, but he believed Mr. Edwards was in denial. Despite the man's formal exterior, inside he must be in torment.

"Mr. Edwards," Tom said softly.

Edwards looked up, his expression fixed.

"I'm going to leave now," he said simply. And he did.

Although at some level Tom had expected this

reaction, he still was startled and he jumped up, trying to call Edwards back. But he was indeed gone.

Tom sat again at his desk, the realization of what he'd just done setting in. He had allowed himself to forget the client, allowed himself to think of his own marriage, his own wife. God, when Edwards had said "Judith," he'd actually thought he'd said "Joan." Yes, he'd allowed his personal life to intrude into the therapeutic setting and as a result he had lost his focus. He had confronted Edwards when the patient wasn't ready. He reviewed his recent blunders, with Emily, with Elizabeth, and now with Edwards. His personal life was taking a toll on his professional life and he knew now, for sure, that he needed to take measures.

He tried to calm himself, to consider ways he could remedy the damage. It was, he finally decided, imperative that he return some control to his client. Difficult as it was, he would wait to see if Edwards came for his regularly scheduled appointment the following week. If he did not, only then would he take steps to encourage him not to terminate.

CHAPTER
—— 13 ——

JAMES DROVE MORE slowly as he approached
Tom's office in Dundrum at mid-day on Thursday. He was stuck in traffic, but, as he admitted
to himself, that wasn't the only thing that was
bothering him. Although he'd developed a feeling
of trust toward Darcy, he was uneasy at the
prospect of talking about himself even one more
time. He resolved to follow through on this session and then politely put the whole therapeutic
relationship on hold.

"Come," Tom said simply, after James arrived
and had barely sat in the chair in the waiting
room. James secretly had mixed feelings. He
would have liked to have seen at least one of
Tom's other clients, out of some morbid sense of
curiosity and also, as he realized suddenly, out
of some distorted sense of possessiveness. On the
other hand, he was still shy of seeing another
client, pondering what he would do if he and the

other person recognized each other. After all, Dublin was a notoriously small town when it came to certain circles.

James was silent as he glanced at Tom's bland face. How could I have felt such affection, James thought angrily. But like an idle thought it was quickly replaced by others.

Tom was silent.

James was annoyed.

Tom leaned forward slightly, his manner less inscrutable. He inclined his head slightly. Was there a hint of a smile? He lifted his eyebrows in a barely perceptible movement.

"Don't you have any other clients, or patients or whatever?" James snapped.

"Why do you ask?"

"How is it that I don't see anyone when I arrive?" James stopped himself with the thought that perhaps Tom scheduled his patients with time to spare, just so they would not meet each other. Yet the thought lingered that perhaps Tom wasn't any good, had no clients. James clenched his fist in an unconscious gesture of irritation, for if Tom had lots of patients it meant he wasn't exclusively interested in him.

"It's a struggle, isn't it?" Tom said softly.

"What is?"

"I am suggesting that you are trying to sort out feelings of jealousy on the one hand, and on the other hand a strong desire perhaps not to commit?"

James's face reddened.

"You're experiencing in our therapeutic relationship feelings that have occurred in other relationships in your life. One of those feelings is not wanting to share *me*. Who else is there in your life, do you think, whom you do not want to share with others?"

James glanced up quickly. "My very first thought?" he said, a tone of surprise in his voice.

"Yes, definitely."

"Okay, then, when you said that—about sharing, I immediately thought of Sarah. But why Sarah? Why not Geraldine?" James ruminated as Tom waited.

"Go on, please."

"Sarah is on tour now, but that's nothing new." James was bitter.

"Does this tour have a significance for you, beyond her not being here in Dublin?" Tom leaned forward.

"I think perhaps it does." James felt a sense of insight pushing him to speak. "I think I resent her displaying herself."

"Displaying?"

"Yes, sharing herself with hundreds, even thousands of people—by the end of one of her long tours. You know, the first time I saw her was at the National Concert Hall right here in Dublin. Do you know it?"

"Yes, after all it was part of UCD when I was a student."

"Right, of course." He continued, "Well, I was dumbfounded by her. She is striking in a certain way, very thin and very fair; her hair is fair and pale, like her skin. She wears it up when she

plays. Her arms and hands are thin and seem
delicate, yet I know they are so incredibly strong
from the endless hours of bowing, and fingering,
of practicing and performing. But she looks ethereal. She is, in many ways, ethereal. She drifts
like smoke in and out of my life and I can't cap-
ture her."

"Like a ghost perhaps?"

"Oh, no," James snapped. "She can be very
corporeal." He glanced quickly at Tom. "Well,
perhaps not very. I admit I would have to
describe her as elusive." James sought hard for
the right words, not only as a well-trained and
experienced lawyer but also as a man desperate
to make another understand him now. "I love
Sarah. I'm not sure she loves me or ever loved
me. There was a time when we were at the point
of marriage. I think I mentioned before I had
bought a house . . ." James fell silent.

"And then?"

"Two things. I became heavily involved in a
case, the case that had brought me in contact
with that artistic community. I can say this in
confidence?"

"Of course."

"You might remember when the rector died in
mysterious circumstances?"

Tom nodded, his eyes inward turning, as if to
acknowledge that the case, widely covered in the
papers, was one of the reasons he had decided to
retain James. "No need to elaborate."

"That case came between us, or rather my
heavy involvement did. I still own the house,

though. I've let it to a very nice couple, both arti-
sans, potters in fact. It's been a while since I was
down there." He stopped again. "Anyway," he
sighed, "round about that time she had a chance
to go on tour and she jumped at it. Good timing.
Bad timing. Who can say?"

"You resented that?"

"Of course. She . . . she abandoned me, I suppose you would say." James looked pointedly at
Tom.

"This house though. You and Sarah had no
plans to live there? Do you now?"

"Humph, I've no plans with Sarah! I have no
plans with Geraldine. The very corporeal Geraldine wants more from me." James was startled at
the jump he'd made from Sarah to Geraldine.

"More than you can give?"

James paused.

"She wants certainty, in that she wants marriage and a home, and a family eventually."

"And you?"

"I want all that. Of course, doesn't everyone?"

Tom's face was expressionless.

"All right," he said almost angrily. "I don't
want to be alone, that's what it is. Never again
alone." James's brow was perspiring and Tom
realized the effort this phrase had cost him.

"What will happen if you are alone? What happens now when you are alone?" he asked softly.

"Nothing really." James waved his long hands
in an impatient gesture.

"Nothing, is that what you are afraid of? Nothing?"

James was aware of the laden nature of the word. Tom was turning it to reveal something to him.

"Nothingness, I suppose. It's the emptiness inside, the hollowness. I have friends, acquaintances, some family ties. My mother calls me daily." James smiled ruefully. "But we're not close. I want, I want that feeling of . . ."

"Of?"

"Of not being alone in the world. You know what it's like—you're at a gathering, a party, anything, a wedding, a funeral, surrounded by people, and you suddenly feel: no one here knows me, really knows me? You feel isolated. It can rush over you . . ." James glanced at Tom's face and saw there a mirror of his own.

Tom nodded.

"I want—not to feel that."

"And you believe that perhaps Sarah, or possibly Geraldine, can make you feel *not alone?*"

"I think so, I've thought so on and off, over the last few years. Now I don't know. I imagine that's why I am here. Really." James looked at Tom frankly, aware that he might have hit on the real issue that was troubling him.

Tom nodded. "All right, then tell me how this affects you physically?"

"Physically, you mean sex?" James exclaimed. "I've had relations with Sarah, and with Geraldine. Though not with Sarah for a long time. And now Geraldine and I are quarreling—there's a tension there."

"No, not sex, believe it or not. Just tell me

what it feels like physically when you are alone,
or have that sense of being alone, even in a
crowd."

James reflected. "Well, it is hard to describe.
Sometimes there's an empty feeling in my stomach. If I am alone in the flat, or a hotel, I can feel
restless . . . almost uneasy in my own skin. Television, radio, tapes, CDs don't help. Exercise does
it, takes my mind off of it. And of course work.
Work, I suppose, has been my antidote."

"Your conveyancing, property, that sort of
thing?"

"To a degree. I think, though, that the private
cases have been more meaningful to me." James
looked up, unsure whether to continue.

"It's all right," Tom answered his unasked
questions. "I am keeping our business and professional relationships quite separate."

"The cases have rung some bell for me,
affected me at my core. I haven't always been a
great success, but I have felt that I've helped people, people who somehow resembled me—isn't
that an odd way to put it? I'm not sure how it is I
came to say that. The people I've met in the cases
had an answering loneliness . . ." James shook his
head as he remembered Ariadne, and Conroy
too, clients who had died violently during his
investigations.

"Is that mirroring loneliness what draws you
to Sarah?"

"Yes."

"Is that what draws you to Geraldine?"

"No, it's the opposite."

Tom was silent and James was stunned at what he was realizing.

"Go on."

"Can't you tell me, can't you help me choose?"

"No. Go on. Work it through."

"Surely if Sarah and I . . ." James sighed heavily. "Surely if we are alike then we would be successful together, as a couple I mean. Geraldine, she's so positive and optimistic. There's no hidden well of loneliness there." James's expression was sorrowful.

"Perhaps it's going to be neither woman."

"Pardon?"

"I said, perhaps in the end it will be neither."

"Oh, Tom! No. I cannot go through this with someone else. I have had long relationships of different natures with both Sarah and Geraldine. Different histories, different events. Both romances have been complicated, mainly by the cases I've come into which involved both of them. I am not in the position to go out there and meet a third person and try again, start again! No."

"All right." Tom's voice was calming. "I'll just observe this. It strikes me when you are speaking that your tie to Sarah is the stronger of the two. Talk to me about that."

"Yes, you're right. But I don't know why that is." Tom was silent.

"Right, then," James said with some anger. "I'll say it out loud. I feel guilty, very guilty over Sarah."

"Why?"

"In the course of the case involving her family it came out in a very limited way that she wasn't the natural child of the elderly couple she had believed to be her parents. Up to then she had led a very privileged life as an only child. And her great musical gift had been carefully nurtured. She lived in a world apart in a sense. Then she learned that she was the daughter of two very ordinary young people, both from farming families. They had never married. She sees herself differently now, and yet presents herself in the same way."

"She resents the reality of her biological background?"

"Yes, she's a snob in a way. But she grew up in a very rarefied atmosphere." James was defensive.

"You feel guilty for being the instrument of revealing all this to her?"

"Yes, she makes me feel guilty. She has some way about her. At the same time, I'm one of the very few people in the world who know her real background, so I imagine she feels safe with me. And in addition to all of that, it was because of me she inherited an enormous fortune that keeps her independent."

"James, at a certain deeper level, you are saying you owe it to Sarah in some way to stay with her, to make it work, perhaps to marry her. It keeps her secret and relieves your guilt. And it is the shame on the one hand and the guilt on the other which bind you together."

"Oh, that sounds pretty bad." James looked stricken.

"People get married for less." Tom smiled gently. There was a long silence. "It seems you are feeling real pressure to decide between them. You expressed that they are both waiting for you to decide."

"Oh, yes! Geraldine with her ultimatum answering Sarah's ultimatum."

Tom was thoughtful for a while and the silence was comfortable.

"Well, James, you're right." Tom studied James's face. "They deserve answers so that they can get on with their lives."

James sighed. "I agree. I am going to work on this. But you know, Tom, when I think about it from their points of views, I don't know why either of them would want a moody bastard like me."

"Oh, you have your good points." Tom smiled, indicating that their time for that session was at an end. And, although reluctant at first, he agreed to James's request for another appointment late the following afternoon.

James was shaken by his session, but as he pulled out of the car park his spirits inexplicably lifted. He felt a surge of affection for Darcy, and for the world at large, and he glanced benignly at his fellow drivers, at pedestrians, even at traffic lights. As he passed the turn that led toward his mother's home, he abruptly decided to visit her. Knowing better than to call ahead, he instead phoned through to Maggie at the office to say he would be a little late. She was about to criticize him in her usual caustic way, but praised him instead when he said he would be at his mother's.

Relieved that Donald's surgery was clearly closed, James walked up the short path to his mother's charming home. Pressing the bell, he waited, calm and full of an affection for her that he hadn't felt in years, or so it seemed.

His affable, amiable mood was penetrated a little when he heard the yelps and whines which were the response to the sound of the bell. He struggled manfully to maintain his mood as high-pitched shrieks alternated with the ever escalating barking. James felt the cords in his neck tighten as he listened as first one and then another of the locks on the other side of the door was unlatched or turned.

"Wait, halloo!" his mother called out.

James didn't bother to reply, knowing it would be drowned out.

"Mack, shush! Mack, now. Good boy!"

"Who is it?" his mother's voice called out, as if the effort was too great to try to open the door.

"It's me. James."

"James?"

"Yes, James. You know. James!" He felt his irritation getting a grip.

"Oh. All right."

The barking continued as Mrs. Fleming opened the door suddenly. Yet as suddenly the door closed again as the chain snapped it back.

"Mother," James growled, the level of his voice now matching the deep noises coming from what sounded like a yelping pack of beagles. He became aware of the next-door neighbor watching across the intervening hedge.

"Hello, Sam." He tried to smile as normally as possible at the elderly man. "It's James," he said despairingly as the man peered at him.

At last the door was flung open and Mack, Mrs. Fleming's pug, attacked his feet, his Italian leather shoes, and the ends of his pure wool trousers. He shook a leg, trying to shake off the dog, whose rotund body wriggled with joy. For the attack wasn't defensive, it was an expression of the dog's undiluted love of humanity—all of it.

"Mack," he cried in exasperation as he stumbled through the door into the hall to be greeted by his mother in her dressing gown.

"James, this is a very awkward time to visit."

James began to feel his mood deteriorating, but he held on valiantly.

"Well, Mother, I really just wanted to see you. How about a cup of tea?"

"Nothing changes." Mrs. Fleming sighed a huge sigh. "Tea, always, tea. You'll have to put the kettle on. I'll just change into my day clothes."

James, knowing well this would take considerable time as she chose a "frock," as she insisted on calling her made-to-order dresses, and selected amongst her vast collection of jewelry what she would deign to wear that day, put a hand on her arm. "No, honestly, you're fine as you are. Let's talk while the kettle boils." James sprinted into the kitchen, plugged in the electric kettle, and grabbed two mugs from their hooks. Carefully rewashing them, he set them on a tray with sugar and poured some milk into another clean mug.

His mother was annoyed as she saw the array

on the tray he brought into the front sitting room. "James, you're hopeless. Now Donald—"

"No, nope, I don't want to hear about Donald today." If at all, he added silently to himself.

"James, this behavior is bizarre. You are frightening me." Mrs. Fleming threw her head dramatically against the back of the tall winged chair in which she sat, oblivious of the magazines scattered on the floor, and oblivious to the large cat that prowled among them looking hopefully as ever for a few crumbs.

"Don't be silly, Mother," James said, checking his irritation just in time.

"But we speak daily. This sudden visit." She sat up and fixed him with her small blue eyes. "Do you have news? Are you getting married!"

James slumped in his chair, but was saved from answering by the whistle of the kettle. On his return he found his mother on her newly acquired cell phone.

"No, truly I can't speak right now. James is here. Yes, James. So pleasant how he drops in like this. We have our little fireside chats, you know. He comes bearing trays of tea for his darling mother. Yes, dear, yes I will phone as soon as he leaves. I know, with his news. Of course."

James bristled. "Mother, I'm here ten minutes and you are broadcasting misinformation. I am not getting married."

"Ever?" his mother shrieked at him.

"I am not even engaged, Mother. Look, I will tell you this." He drew a deep breath, trying to put into action some barely discernible resolve he'd made in the car. "I am going to get my life on track. I am giving a lot of thought to my situation, you know, with Sarah and with—"

"Oh, that country girl. Don't mention her to me."

"Mother, you must get past this issue of religion. Sarah is Catholic as well."

"I know, but no one suspects. She is so very refined, and famous."

James sighed as he sipped the tea. It wasn't very good but his mother didn't seem to notice.

"Work is going well, and I am involved in a private case which is very interesting. Sarah actually is away right now, and Geraldine"— James ignored his mother's snort—"is busy at the hospital. And well, I've been doing a lot of thinking. In fact, I've gone to one or two therapy sessions." He waited for the outburst.

"Very trendy, dear." Mrs. Fleming reached for the plate of biscuits he'd left for her.

"Pardon?"

"Mrs. Bailey's going, and Mrs. Thing-me down the road, her husband is going. And I heard from Beverly that her son is going. It's really the 'done thing' right now. You were always just a little behind, you know, dear, behind the trends. Donald, now—"

"It's very helpful," James cut in, but his enthusiasm for making contact with his mother was fast sagging under the weight of her own preoccupations.

"Good, dear, good. Now if you would just feed Mack, I'll run along upstairs."

James wandered into the kitchen searching for something to appease the rotund beige figure at his feet. He glanced down into Mack's round black eyes and observed the comical tilt of his head. His long pink awry tongue stuck out in anticipation of any goodies James might offer. Dutifully James fed the dog, and the cat too, and washed up the tea things and hung the towel on the rack. The kitchen, like the rest of the house, like Mack's tongue, was completely awry, but this time, for the first time, James just shrugged and left it.

He met his mother in the hall as she rummaged in her capacious purse for her keys. She looked well in her blue flowered dress, her ample bosom bedecked with a brooch the size of a small county.

"Off so soon, James? Too bad. I know your work calls. I'm off as well. There's a tour of a garden at Enniskerry; they're calling it 'autumnal antics.' Is that not quaint? And Mrs. Browne tells me there is a luncheon laid on, included in the price."

James bent to kiss her but she shifted just in time.

"Right, I'm off then," he said a bit forlornly.

As he walked toward his car, she called after him: "You know, James, I do so prefer Sarah. Cheerio!"

CHAPTER
14

Tom was waiting in the sitting room when Joan finally returned late Thursday night. The hastily scribbled note, which she'd left lying on the kitchen table, hadn't impressed him: pointing him as it did toward the freezer and the microwave. He'd had no appetite.

It had been the sense that someone was following him home to his house that had truly unnerved him. He had actually found himself going in at the side door, found himself running to the front sitting room to peer through the curtains to see if there was anyone there, perhaps a car. There had been a car, parked across the road. But there had been no driver, no one to be seen. The car meant nothing, he assured himself. To settle his nerves he'd poured himself a very large brandy and then, as the minutes ticked away, another.

Tom was in very bad form when he heard Joan's car pulling into the driveway. He waited as

he heard her key, as he heard her high heels click
on the kitchen floor, as he heard her calling out
his name, a little hesitantly, since the house,
including the sitting room, was still in darkness.
Joan came almost reluctantly into the living
room when he finally answered, and she
switched on the lamp.

"Tom! What are you doing in the dark?"

"Where were you?" he said without preamble

"What?"

"Where were you?"

Joan heard the icy coldness in his voice.

"I was out."

"Clearly."

"On a date."

The hair on the back of his neck rose. He knew
they'd had problems, he admitted that to himself,
but this? Had he been so stupid, so blind over
these last months? Had his own preoccupations
prevented him from picking up on the underlying
signals that she was actually seeing another man?

"With whom?"

"George."

"How long has this been going on?" he said
angrily.

"I don't know. We've been friends for quite a
while."

"Friends?" Tom's voice was level now.

"We've worked together from the beginning at
Foy's."

Foy's was the large real estate agency that Joan
had joined when she had decided to return to
work. Christopher, their son, had been gone a

few years, to California, to pursue a career in advertising. Tom had been saddened when his son had got one of the American visas in the lottery. He had been disappointed in his choice of career, in fact by many of his son's choices, but he had said very little. Joan, he knew, had been devastated. Her only child, so far away. And if Chris married out there . . . She used to cry about it. It had taken weeks, even months, before she adjusted to their son's absence. Perhaps she never had.

He himself had thought it would be a time to renew their marriage. Christopher had lived at home during his years at the university. Even though it was a large house Tom was always conscious of his presence, his comings and goings. Tom had anticipated enjoying being alone again with his wife. But why? he wondered now, as he heard her voice.

"Don't you remember him?"

"Of course not. Why should I?"

"That's really you, Tom, isn't it," said Joan as she sat on the edge of the blue upholstered chair. "You've met him, you know, at the Christmas parties. But you don't like parties, do you, Tom." Joan's voice was thick with sarcasm. "You dread going and complain after we leave. I realized you were a loner, Tom, after a few years, but it's got worse, much worse."

"That's ridiculous. I'm, as they say, a people person," he snapped, emphasizing the last words.

"No, you are a work person. It's your patients that you care about. Only them. No one else matters. Not Christopher, not me, not our few friends, actually not even yourself."

"What's that supposed to mean?"

"All right, I'll tell you. This is what it is like. You leave for work; we barely exchange words in the morning. And you don't just work nine to five, sometimes you work eight to eight, or nine to nine, depending on your clients and their bloody needs—oh, how I hate that word."

"That's what I do, Joan."

"Alone all day with these disturbed people, talking, listening, talking, listening. And then when you get home you're drained, so you have a few drinks and watch television and go to bed. And the weekends are a real joy: you sleep late because you're so tired. You catch up on your reading, do a few things around the house . . ."

"And on Sundays you are not here because you are out showing houses!"

"Because I couldn't stand the weekends, Tom, the boredom. Christ!"

"Oh, Joan."

"What? Do we take vacations or do you golf or attend conferences in Ibiza or anywhere else for godsakes, like other medical men? Oh God no, that would be normal, sociable, friendly."

"You mean like your father?"

"Yes, yes I do. He had a good life as a surgeon, a very good life. And so did we, mother and the rest of us. That wasn't a crime."

"I'm good at what I do."

"Why couldn't you be a regular psychiatrist then, attached to the hospital, instead of this self-indulgent little kingdom, this private practice that you have. Honestly, I don't know how you justify your existence to yourself. You are a physician, Tom. Physicians save lives. What do you do?"

Tom was wounded to the core, so deeply he couldn't look at the face of his wife of twenty-five years.

"And this gives you the right to go out on a date? Did you kiss?" he asked her at last.

"Yes," said Joan evenly.

"Oh, I see," said Tom, his voice rising. "And did you sleep with him too?"

"No, but we are thinking about it."

"We?"

"Yes. Look, this isn't a surprise, Tom. I mentioned a separation, even a divorce to you before. It was you who chose not to take me seriously."

Tom felt that the throbbing in his head must be audible, that the heat coursing through his body must be visible, like the red steam that rose off cartoon characters when they were angry. He tried to remain calm, but he had lost his composure.

"Was he following me tonight?"

"Pardon?"

"Has he been following me, playing pranks . . ."

"Oh God!"

"No, I'm serious. What do you know about this man?"

"He's not crazy. Honestly, Tom, listen to yourself. You are with sick people all day long. It's affecting your thinking!" Joan stood up to retrieve her cigarettes from her bag.

"But how do you know? I'm asking you seriously. What do you know about him?"

"He loves me, that's what I know," she cried, throwing the packet across the room. "And you don't."

Tom was not giving up.

"Tell me about him, Joan, tell me."

"No, I won't. I've never seen you like this. You're the one who's acting crazy."

"Shut up, Joan," Tom said coldly, her use of the loaded word goading him.

But Joan was laughing at him now. He tried with effort to regain some composure.

"Look, Joan. What exactly have I done to you? It's not my fault that Christopher moved to California. But you blame me. I've worked all our married life at work I am good at. I've given all of us a pretty good life. I don't drink much. I haven't run around. I've never had an affair. When your . . ."

"Oh please, stop, just stop."

"I'm serious, Joan. I hear . . ." Tom hesitated, afraid of his own thoughts. "I think I hear hatred in your voice."

But Joan interrupted, her expression contorted with rage.

"Hate. Yes, I have felt hate. But I'll tell you what's worse. I don't like you anymore, Tom."

"God, Joan." Sadness overwhelmed him. Hurt and dismay surged through him.

"How do I know you haven't had affairs? Tell me that. I think you have. I think you've been in love with your patients for years. They are your life. Admit it. It's all you think about, even when you're home, or with me, or having sex. Your goddamned patients. Even now, there's someone special, don't deny it. I always knew it, all these years."

"Knew what?"

"I always knew when there was one, a special one."

Tom stood up, running his fingers through his hair. Even as she had spoken he'd seen Emily in his mind. It was just fantasy, he knew that. Of course. Fantasy. He'd never acted on it. But he knew, as he breathed deeply, that he shouldn't have allowed even that much to enter his thoughts.

Joan was continuing now, spilling out the rage she'd apparently been bottling up for months.

"Oh, you might not be sleeping with her yet, but you will in due course. And while you are waiting for her to give in—"

"Jesus, that's enough, Joan. You don't know me at all, even after all these years. After twenty-five years. I've never had an affair with a patient. I'd lose my license."

"Is that the only reason?"

"No, of course not. I just wouldn't do it, how could you think it? It's against everything I believe in."

"Oh, our marriage vows."

"No, not only those vows, not that they are stopping you. But my own oath, as a physician, and as a therapist—my own code of ethics would prevent me. I'd destroy the patient and myself in the process, if I ever had an affair. I could never

practice again as a therapist. It is the single thing
I can never do."

"Aha, you are protesting too much. I see from
that, there is someone. You've confirmed it now.
Who is she? Some frail little delicate female,
hanging on your every word, running to you
once a week to pour out her heart. What is it? Is
she lonely? Is her husband a brute? Doesn't he
understand her the way you do, dear Dr. Darcy."

"Stop it, I say."

"Only you can save her, Dr. Darcy."

"Well she hasn't put on weight, I can tell you
that. And she doesn't smoke or drink. And she
can carry on an intelligent conversation." Tom
hurled the words at her and they hit.

Joan sat down suddenly. The room was deadly
calm.

Tom sat down too.

"Joan, this is pure fantasy. I'll just say this: I've
never been involved with a patient. You can put
that from your mind. Now, I'm tired, I've had a
few brandies. Not that any of this is an excuse.
I'm angry, I lost control. Look, I am sorry, Joan."
He looked at her, his appeal for peace written on
his face.

"I don't believe you," she said simply.

Tom stopped abruptly, fatally.

"I've never been unfaithful—"

"Oh, yes you have, Tom. You've been unfaithful in your imagination. How dare you challenge
me about George."

"George, yes, I remember him now." Tom felt
weakened.

"He's a lot of fun, and handsome. And he kisses well too. He makes me feel good . . ." Joan was taunting again.

Tom sat very still, his head spinning.

"He makes me feel young. I look forward to seeing him, like a girl with her first love."

Tom pressed his hands to the side of his head, calming his thoughts, trying not to hear her, trying in vain to regain some self-control. It was a struggle. He could hear her walking across the room and pouring herself a drink. He knew now she wanted to keep the argument going, to provoke him. But why? To relieve her own guilt? He heard the sound of her voice but no longer did he listen to the vituperative words. The pounding in his head stopped and he took a deep breath.

Finally he stood up, clearly startling her.

Calm once again, he spoke softly. "Joan, please, just, just wait a minute. I don't think this is healthy. It's late, we are both overwrought. What I suggest is we call a truce for now, maybe get some rest?"

She merely stared at him, holding her drink to her mouth.

"Well, I'll head upstairs," he said it neutrally.

"Don't bother sleeping in our bed. If you do, I'll sleep in the guest room." She spat out the words.

Tom turned away as from a blow. "Fine. But I'll tell you now, Joan, a divorce is out of the question." He didn't stay to wait for her reaction.

Upstairs, in the large cold unused guestroom, he pulled the covers back from the bed. The colorful bright flowers on the shiny surface of the mattress glared up at him. No sheets. No blankets. With a terrible sense of inevitability he pulled off his shoes, then his suit, and threw himself across the bed.

The loneliness was complete, the loneliness he'd fought all his life, which he had kept at bay through university, through his medical training, through all these latter years as he knew himself to be getting older. He'd fought so hard and now, now he'd lost. Utter, overwhelming emptiness faced him now. He closed his eyes against the void.

CHAPTER
—— 15 ——

DR. TOM DARCY stood beside Mary's narrow hospital bed in the private room at St. Patrick's Psychiatric Hospital as the sounds of the early morning routine went on around them. It had been quite a while since one of his patients had had to be hospitalized, and as he looked down at her troubled face he felt an overwhelming sense of failure. It had been only hours since he'd seen her in his office and yet here she was and here he was. As she turned her face to him at last, he drew a chair close to the bed, near to her head, so that he could hear her softly spoken words.

"Mary, Mary, can you tell me what happened? Please, as best you can . . ."

Mary struggled to remember. And the memories came, slowly at first, and then in a rush.

"Talk to me, please."

His voice was soothing and the sheets on the bed were cool and stiff. She stretched and relaxed for the first time in what felt like years. She felt safe here in this white, cool room.

"When I left your office I had some difficulty getting the car started. It was like I couldn't concentrate, or that I was distracted."

Mary continued talking to Tom, in a narrative voice, almost as though she were remembering a series of events that had happened to someone she knew.

Slowly, she recounted how she had picked up her son at his junior school on Thursday afternoon and listened without hearing to the trials and tribulations of his six-year-old life. Smiling vacantly she let him into the house and poured him a glass of milk.

She remembered thinking that he was looking at her with a puzzled expression, but she put it out of her mind. Switching on the television set, she put him in front of it wordlessly and then lay on the sofa, hearing nothing, seeing only the trees moving outside the window.

It was October now, leaves were starting to drop in increasing numbers. The sycamores across the road waved their thin top branches to her as if in recognition of the many hours they had watched her lying in that very spot, prone, motionless, without the will to move.

She told Tom how she had tried, really tried. She had made a plan. At half three she would get up and make the beds, only two beds. That wasn't bad. She could do that. In fact it would only take five minutes. That meant she could wait until four. She didn't need to look at the clock on the mantel. She could tell time by the change of the programs on the television. Her son was in the room. She turned her head slightly to see him. He was sprawled, sucking his thumb. She knew he was too old to suck his thumb. She acknowledged that to herself. And now to Tom.

At four o'clock she thought she would get up. If she made the beds she'd feel better, and then she could clear the table, put the breakfast things away. And, she thought, if she did that much, then the table would be clear for the evening meal. She had bought chops one day. Were they still good?

At five she raised her head to tell her son to switch on the lamp and the light in the hall. Brian would be coming in at six. He liked to see the light on in the hall. She felt that the chops were probably bad. Pork was a risk. She could still make the beds. No. But she could still clear the table. No. There were some microwave meals in the freezer.

She asked her son to look in the top part of the fridge and come back and tell Mummy if there were some meals. He was gone so long she'd forgotten why he was standing beside her, saying something.

At six she heard Brian's key in the lock, she heard him call her name. She hadn't noticed when the window beyond the pale curtains had turned completely black. She couldn't see the treetops now.

She heard the irritation in Brian's voice as he asked what was for bloody dinner. She heard the plates slam on the kitchen table as he asked again what she did all day. She saw his shoes, as he stood beside her. Brown shoes. Scuffed. They didn't go with the black suit he'd worn to work.

Slowly, as if heaving a great weight before her, she had got up. How could feeling hollow make one so heavy, she asked Tom now from the safety of the clean white bed. Her limbs had been so heavy.

She remembered she was in the kitchen. The overhead light made it all seem strangely yellow. She braced her hands on the sink and tried to think.

Take the meals from the freezer. She sent from some distant reaches of her brain a message to her body. There were no meals in the freezer. Despair caught at her chest. The hollowness was moving, from the pit of her stomach up, up through her chest, to her throat.

Brian had found her kneeling with her head against the fridge door. She brushed his helping hands away and stood. With an almighty act of will she took out tins of stew. She watched as Brian and their son ate at the table that Brian had cleared. She saw their lips moving and heard faint sounds. She nodded and smiled once, at least. She saw stew on her plate. It was very far away. She waited as long as she could. The effort was excruciating. Five more minutes and she could leave. Four. Yes, she had to lie down now. No, she felt quite well. She just had to lie down now.

In the sitting room she lay on the sofa, moving images passed across the screen. She knew it was coming. The endless day would soon be over. She had seen the nightgown on the floor. She pulled it on over her clothes and then kicked off her shoes.

At last relief flooded through her. Tomorrow would be better. She would clean in the morning. Perhaps go to the shops. She'd make the beds. She'd clear the table . . .

She didn't remember coming to the hospital. Could Tom tell her, please?

Tom was more than puzzled by Mary's intractable depression. She worried him more than he cared to admit, he realized, as he spoke with the nurse who was on duty. He'd had to tell her that her husband, Brian, had phoned him, anger in his voice masking fear and utter bewilderment. Where was the girl he'd married? he'd demanded. Tom had had no answers.

He stepped into the office the physicians used when attending to patients they had admitted, and began to write his notes in Mary's folder. But he put his pen down, discouraged. He'd tried, so hard, to empathize with Mary, to get near to her in her depression. He'd dug deep into his own experience, the depressions he'd endured over the years himself, but he couldn't seem even to approximate hers. It was, as she said herself, always there, waiting, like a dark body of water all around her, just out of sight but there all the same. Waiting. Ever present. Threatening. And now it had overtaken her.

Her depression now was absolutely exquisite, like a carefully wrought Celtic pattern. The hollowness was so complete—how could he possibly fill it, even briefly, even temporarily, to give her some relief? Was it a gender difference? he mused, and he picked up his pen again. He did not think so, but perhaps there was something unique, so integral to her being female that there was no way for him to understand it. No. He shook the thought away. "Nothing human is alien to me," he murmured the classical phrase. He would keep trying.

Tom reviewed the medication he'd prescribed for her during the last six months. He'd used a second-generation and usually successful antidepressant, and she had claimed it helped. Well, it was back to the drawing board. He knew he would read the newest journals when he got home that night; perhaps phone a psychopharmacologist he knew fairly well. Making his final notes, he stood and closed the folder. At least Mary was safe, in a place where she could be monitored. Her husband had felt relieved at that too, despite his anger at Tom, anger that had dissipated into fear.

Tom walked slowly down the corridor with a sense of something menacing. Mary had taken his attention, but he realized he was feeling something anticipatory, some apprehension about the new client he would be seeing later that day. Suddenly restless, he glanced at his watch. A good hard ride on Quixote before he went to the office would be so . . .

Oh . . .

CHAPTER
——16——

JOAN HAD BEEN waiting, sitting in her living room, staring through the sheer white curtains out at the road. As a car turned the bend, she jumped, relieved and apprehensive at once. But after an hour had passed and no one had pulled up to her house, she phoned her husband.

"Tom?" she said as his message clicked on the voice-recording machine at his office. "It's Joan. Pick up, for heavens' sake. You agreed to talk tonight and now it's an hour beyond the time you selected, if I can remind you of that." She stopped, getting control of her voice. "Tom?" she said again. "Give me a ring as soon as you get this message." She slammed down the receiver. It was important now that she not waver. Fundamentally, she said half aloud, Tom had always been in the wrong.

Darkness had fallen and she closed the drapes over the curtains. As more time passed, she went to the Rolodex on the hallstand. Quickly locating

Mrs. Fogarty's home number, she phoned her.
Sharp and to the point, she asked when Dr.
Darcy planned to come home.

"Why, Mrs. Darcy, this is Friday."

"I'm well aware of that."

"I only work in the mornings on Fridays. I
stayed a bit longer today—"

"I'm sure you did," Mrs. Darcy replied sarcasti-
cally, and regretted it when she was met with
silence.

"I wasn't there this afternoon," Mrs. Fogarty
finally spoke. "But usually his last appointment
is at four on a Friday." Mrs. Fogarty had a note of
possessiveness in her tone.

"Then it doesn't make sense. He'd finish at five
and be home by six."

"Why, it's just half six now," Mrs. Fogarty said
calmly. "Perhaps—"

"But we had an appoint— I mean I thought we
were going to meet at six." Joan was too abrupt.

"And he hasn't rung you?" Was that sarcasm?
Joan wondered.

"No—it's all right," she added hastily. "I'm sure
he's on his way."

Mrs. Fogarty reluctantly hung up, as Joan cut
her off with the perfunctory apology for bothering her.

As Joan strode purposefully to her car, Mrs.
Fogarty, in her own much more modest home,
settled her two children in front of the television
set. Their father was already off for the evening,
down the corner at the local pub, spending, she
thought bitterly, the equivalent of the money she

had earned that week at Dr. Darcy's. But it was her money, and her drunk of a husband couldn't get at it, she thought with a little satisfaction as she changed back into her street clothes and looked for her handbag. She carefully checked her makeup. She'd known all along, she said silently to the face in the mirror, there had been trouble in that marriage. Now she'd heard it confirmed in Mrs. Darcy's voice tonight. What a foolish woman, Mrs. Fogarty said aloud. Dr. Darcy was so handsome, so sensitive and kind, and, of late, so very, very sad. Mrs. Fogarty told the kids again that their father was down the corner, and she locked her door and walked quickly to her car. It wasn't far—she'd be back and forth to the office in a jiffy.

Joan was relieved to see, when she pulled into the car park, that there were lights on in the building. She ran up the ramp, through the heavy outside door and past the first office on the ground floor. Their door was open and she glanced in, waving to the cleaning lady who was hoovering loudly. Moving quickly she went to the outer door of her husband's suite of offices.

Now that she was there, she hesitated. Drawing breath, she turned the knob and went in. The heavy door clicked shut behind her. The waiting room was as always, neat and orderly: the lights low, the magazines straightened, Mrs. Fogarty's desk bare and gleaming, the word processor covered. There was no sound but the soft low music on the radio and the small white-noise machine in the corner was purring its annoying sound-deadening whirr. The door to her husband's office was shut. She paused. Yes, that was it! He'd had a late appointment and had forgotten to tell her.

"Tom!" she called, placing her mouth near the doorjamb. "Tom?"

She heard nothing, nor would she have. The door, the office, everything had been arranged for maximum soundproofing—all for the patients' confidentiality. She paused again.

What she saw when she finally pulled open the door would stay with her for the rest of her life.

James was surprised to see so many cars in the parking lot as he pulled the Citroën into one of the spaces just behind the small Fiat that he'd trailed all the way down the main road. He was more surprised to see, as he was forced to slow his steps behind her, that the woman who exited the Fiat was heading in the same direction as he was. She entered the building, and as she glanced apprehensively over her shoulder in his direction, he dropped back, not wanting to frighten her. Yet as he watched her walk purposefully down the corridor, he realized she was heading for Darcy's office too. James was annoyed. Even though he was late for the six o'clock appointment, it was still his time, his time with Darcy. He already regarded his session time selfishly, possessively. He realized to his astonishment that he didn't want to share Darcy with anyone else.

"Two patients scheduled at the same time!" he nearly said aloud, as she entered Darcy's office.

But such random angry thoughts ceased on the moment at the sound of a piercing scream, followed instantly by another, more garbled, filled with words and sobs. Shuddering from head to toe, James ran the last remaining few yards to the office door. Yanking it open, he heard a repeat of the screams—only much louder, and much more desperate.

Crossing the waiting room, he opened the inner door and beheld in an instant a terrifying silent tableau. To his left, standing huddled against the wall, was a woman, her hands covering her face and mouth, but her eyes protruding, staring toward the desk. James's mind refused to register what was on the desk, and instead his gaze moved to another woman, on her knees, bent at the waist, who was rocking back and forth.

As sound finally reemerged into his consciousness he heard as from a great distance a voice calling: "Oh, God, oh God, oh God." This seemed to be coming from the woman on the floor. The woman to his left was gasping, deep raucous grabs for breath that wouldn't come.

Paralyzed into inaction, only able to move his eyes, his vision at last encompassed the body of Dr. Darcy. For months afterward, James remembered seeing first the slight bald spot under the thick gray hair on Tom Darcy's head. Then he saw that the head was lying in a position that was incompatible with life.

A gleaming pool of blood had covered the wide mahogany surface and was dripping down the two sides nearest him. Dark stains were forming on the brown carpet. Horrible to see; so sweet and sickly to smell.

Where were his hands? James wondered, still in shock. He had nice hands, a kind handshake—kind, firm, like his face. If he were asleep his hands would be on the desk. They weren't on the desk.

In a daze, James walked behind the woman on the floor and, approaching the desk, went to see where Tom's hands were. He needed to know that. Horrified and fascinated, he was finally struck by the reality. He bent down to look at Darcy's face. The dead man was lying on his right cheek, eyes open, mouth gaping, muscles slack.

"He's gone," James said aloud, and looked at his watch, noting the time automatically. Tears filled his eyes so quickly they fell onto his wristband. A sudden sob escaped his mouth and heart as he watched his new friend's face in death. He looked for the soft reassuring expression, and not finding it, he despaired.

The cries of the two women were abating. One of them spoke and he snapped back to himself. After all, he said to buck himself up, he'd seen death before, death on the face of a friend before—on a dolmen in the wilds of Sligo.

"I think we all should leave this room," he said brusquely as he helped the woman, whom he would later learn to be Mrs. Fogarty, from her knees.

"I said, who are you?" repeated the other woman, who was still shrinking against the wall.

"Fleming, James Fleming." He looked at her

closely. "Mrs. Darcy?" he said, still supporting the trembling Mrs. Fogarty by the elbow.

"Yes," she answered dully, and moved shakily toward him. Together the three of them went into the waiting room. After he seated them, he opened the door, amazed to hear the droning of the Hoover pouring from the other office, surprised that life was continuing at all, let alone in this same building.

"I'm going to call the police now," he informed the women, taking his cell phone from his pocket. "I'd ask that you stay here and touch nothing."

Quickly making the call, he ran to the neighboring office and told the startled cleaning lady that she too was to remain in the building until the police came. As she protested that she had seen nothing, heard nothing, James was inclined to believe her, but he took note of her name nonetheless.

Then, quietly, with some caution, he went upstairs and ascertained as best he could that the two offices on the upper floor were empty. At least they were locked. If anyone were inside, it would take the police to find out. Racing outside he trotted around the small building. The windows were of the modern style—with no way that an adult could pass through any one of them with their narrow hinged openings designed purposely to prevent break-ins. He noted the cars in the lot—his own, the two BMWs that he assumed were Tom's and his wife's, the Fiat he now knew to belong to Mrs. Fogarty. No other cars. There had been other cars, but he couldn't remember them. Exhausted yet alert, he stood on guard at the front door, but no one approached. Cars passed, slowing and speeding up as the various traffic lights warranted. He looked across the street to a dark and shuttered bank, above that to the trees that sheltered it, and above them to the sky where a few stars were visible.

Tears filled his eyes and nausea and dread filled his soul. Selfish, so selfish, he whispered to himself. His grief for Darcy was grief for himself. Not very admirable, he admitted. He knuckled the tears away. Brutal. Brutal. His stomach churned. He'd rejected what he'd seen until now. The throat cut, the gash so deep the imagination couldn't credit it. He let the sense of loss wash over him, for it was pointless to fight against it. In such a short time he'd felt such warmth, such caring, from Darcy, and he in turn such an affection for him, such a need, yes, a need for him, that he could barely understand it. But now was not the time to grieve—the nee-naw whine of a siren claimed his attention. He glanced at his watch as he had before. Twelve minutes had passed. And now the rest of the ordeal would begin.

CHAPTER
—— 17 ——

G OD, I'M EXHAUSTED," James said as Geraldine stirred beside him.

"You haven't slept at all, have you?" Geraldine asked as he rolled from his back to his side, facing her in the rumpled bed.

"Are you angry with me?"

"Yes," she said simply.

James sat up abruptly and swung his legs over the side of the bed. She could see the tension in his back muscles. He was searching for his clothes.

"I think you might have told me you were coming off a case before we made love, not after."

"Well, I think that that would have been something of a passion-killer," James retorted.

Stung, she stood up and threw on her dressing gown.

"Well, I think you used me."

"Oh, it always gets back to that, doesn't it?"

James pulled on his trousers. "I used you before, yes, but, my God, it was to catch a killer—"

"But Brona was my friend!"

"Yes, and you aren't ever going to let me forget, are you? I've said I am sorry in every way possible—but it's never enough." James fumbled at the buttons on his shirt and gave up, grabbing instead for his suit jacket.

"You know, I didn't use you this morning, Geraldine." James was shouting now, hoarse and tired. "I needed you."

They both stopped in their tracks, stunned by what he'd just said.

"What?"

"You heard me. I needed to make love to you, damn it, I needed to feel you and hold you in the dark. I wanted to feel alive, to push away that blackness. Can't you understand? Don't you know me at all?" James, pale and drawn, lowered his voice. "What am I—a three piece suit to you? The 'lawyer and the doctor'—does it sound good to your friends? Are we a 'couple'? Oh, we've been through so much, Geraldine, we should be beyond all this by now."

"I never liked you doing private cases," Geraldine interjected, trembling from head to toe.

"Oh, what of it—you never liked this, you never liked that. Did I choose this? Yeah, I chose the law, I chose to do real estate, for God's sake, real estate law. Is that what you loved in me? Or maybe you never did . . ."

"Oh, no, I—"

"Oh just stop, will you? I'm sick of all this.

You've got some idea of who I am. Well, I'm not. This is me, yes me, James, warts and all. Maybe it's strange, maybe it doesn't suit your picture, and God knows what that is! You, you of all people. A doctor, for chrissakes. You see death; you've seen death. Well, I've seen death too, Ger. I thought you were different."

"Different?" Ger whispered.

"Yeah, different—not like, not like . . . Sarah." James sagged onto the bed, reaching for his tie. "Sarah—up on stage, Sarah insulated by her music, a hundred light-years away from death and evil."

"I know nothing of evil," Ger shouted, stung by his reference to Sarah.

"Death, is evil, Ger. Death is evil when it comes too early, or when it comes too late." James put his face in his hands.

"Is this some kind of competition, James? If Sarah were here and not me, would you be 'pushing away the blackness' with her?" Her tone was sarcastic.

"Jesus!" James looked up at her, his eyes as stony and hard and cold as hate, and for the first time Geraldine was unnerved.

"James, I'm sorry." She watched as he stood up.

"You don't get it, do you." It was a statement.

"No," she yelled, tears in her eyes.

"I needed you, I wanted you."

"No, I was a body in the dark!"

"Aren't we all—aren't we all just bodies in the dark? Hanging on to something, to each other! You blocked out what I'd seen, you filled the void!"

"I was a body." Geraldine spat out the words.

"You weren't Sarah."

"It doesn't matter."

"I wouldn't have gone to be with Sarah, I wanted to be with you. That's what you don't get. Maybe it's because you are someone who sees death and you go on—you are life, yes, you're life for me. I'm not life, Sarah isn't life—but you were, to me." James grimaced with fatigue.

"Oh, James, I'm sorry. Look, I—"

They looked at each other across what had become a vast expanse of rumpled bedclothes, of yesterday's laundry, of years of hurt and unspoken words, of rivalries and confusion, of unhealed wounds, of lack of trust and misplaced longing. But he was still there and she was still there.

"James, listen, don't go, not yet. I'll make some breakfast, anything you like, coffee at least. You could take a shower. Okay?" She looked at him, waiting.

"Right," he said and left the room.

"I am sorry, James," said Geraldine as they sat at the kitchen table. James had finished recounting the events of the night before. "You said so little when you phoned, and when you got here you were so, well, so . . ." She looked down at her empty cup.

"Driven . . . ?"

"Well, yes," she said, acknowledging their furious and almost wordless physical coupling after his arrival at her flat.

Now, at breakfast, exhaustion descended on them and worked to dull the angry reactions of an hour before.

Ger set the cup aside and lit a cigarette. "I thought it was just another case. Sorry, no. What I mean is—I didn't realize you had come to know him, Darcy, personally. You know what I'm trying to say."

"Well, I didn't let you in on the details of the case. And about the other matter. It's hardly something a man is going to rush to admit—that he's 'in therapy,' as they say." James shrugged.

Geraldine poured more coffee into his cup.

"I had an appointment at six, and I was running late. That's the irony . . . that's why I went there, to Darcy's office, last night." James rubbed his forehead, looking around rather desperately, looking for a touchstone for reality.

"You know, James," Ger said kindly, "if you hadn't, you'd be reading about this in today's papers, or hearing it on the news."

"God, I haven't told you, nor will I, what I saw. It would have been better to hear about this on the news and I am serious about that."

"Come on, now. This has been a terrible shock, but—"

"No, no! You're not listening. I saw what I saw. His injuries were terrible. You don't have to do this. I don't need the pep talk. I was there. And I'll never forget it. The blood, I've never seen anything like it—" He stopped abruptly, stood up and sat down again. Geraldine watched him nervously as he looked around him again.

"What is it?"

"I was going to say, I'd never seen such a pool of blood. But I have. At least in the police photos. When Darcy's horse was killed—"

"I remember—you did tell me that much at the time."

"The blood had pooled under that horse, Darcy's horse!" James shivered at the similarity he was recognizing. He looked up. "But it's starting to make some kind of sense."

"What?"

"The killing of the horse, other things that Darcy mentioned to me, and now his murder. An escalating pattern. This wasn't random violence. There was purpose here. Jesus!"

"What is it, James? What's wrong?"

"Initially I'd been pretty forceful with Darcy. I'd warned him. He had downplayed it. But I should have seen through that. He was diffident always, and refused to believe a patient could do such things."

"You think it was a patient!"

"Isn't it obvious?"

"Well, yes, I suppose, if someone was truly disturbed." Geraldine felt obliged to agree.

James jumped up. "I warned him, but not strongly enough. He'd hired me to help him, and I let him down."

James hesitated. Ger could see the fatigue and sadness, and yes, the guilt she'd seen in his face before, at other times, and other places, and she grew discouraged. Since she'd known him, his cases had brought him great heartache.

"It's all right, James. Go," she whispered.

"What do you mean?" He looked up at her face for the first time in what seemed like hours.

"Go, just go. Do what you have to do."

"Are you sure?"

"Yes, go. Go to the police, or to his house, or wherever it is you have to go." She stood up and straightened the things on the small table. She glanced around her flat and his eyes followed hers. Orderly, bright, cheerful, a medical textbook here, a magazine there. Colorful flowers in a purple vase. James looked at it all with a sense of remoteness, as though he'd been cut off from ordinary human relations. He thought she wanted to embrace him; he wondered what he would do if she did.

"I'll be off then," he said.

"Right," she said, as she put the coffee mugs in the sink. "See you."

Going to his office helped James immeasurably. Although it was Saturday, Walter Poole, one of the best conveyancing men in his firm, was working away in his office. And what truly surprised James was seeing Maggie stride out of his office as he walked in.

"Hey?" he said, actually smiling.

"James, I'm really sorry." She was holding the morning papers in her hands. "When I saw the paper at home this morning I called your flat. I wasn't sure then where you'd be." Despite the gravity of the situation Maggie arched an inquiring eyebrow which James ignored. "I thought I'd come by here. I had odds and ends to do in any case."

"Oh, Maggie," James said too seriously, touched by her concern, and she blushed as she walked away.

"Coffee?"

"Food, please? Oh, and Darcy's home address. It's in—"

"I know."

James changed into the suit he kept at the office, and after eating the food Maggie had left him on a tray, he felt more in command of himself than he had in some hours.

"Thanks, Maggie," he said as he emerged from his office, "for—" James waved his hand to indicate her kindness and loyalty. "Listen, I'm off to see Mrs. Darcy. After that, who knows? But get Whelan on the phone for me, track him down, tell him I'll be phoning. I want his undivided attention until this killer is found."

CHAPTER
—— 18 ——

JAMES WAS SURPRISED when Mrs. Darcy herself opened the door to her home, and more surprised still to find that she was alone.

"Mrs. Darcy. I don't know if you remember me."

"Come in, Mr. Fleming. Of course I remember you—not from last night. But I remember you from handling the purchase of our house."

She led James into the plush sitting room off the entryway. Everything struck him as terribly still and unused, like a show house. He found himself picturing Darcy there and it didn't fit. He didn't like it. This was not Darcy. Tom would have been wood and leather, books and music, Persian rugs and fine wine. And yet, he reminded himself, he'd seen this house before, albeit empty. He'd not had such feelings about it then. He'd met Darcy years before. Why hadn't they become friends then? All the years they would have had. He left the thought unfinished.

He glanced up, embarrassed by his own musings, embarrassed that Joan Darcy had spoken and he hadn't heard.

Looking at him blandly she asked James to sit and offered him a drink, which he gladly accepted. He noticed that she poured them both very large brandies from the decanter on the drinks trolley without asking a preference. She sat tiredly on the sofa and closed her eyes briefly.

He felt at a loss to begin and so waited, feeling stupid and dull.

"What time did you finish?" she asked suddenly.

"Ah, let me see, the police interviewed you first of course. Then when you left, Mrs. Fogarty. Then myself. I waited until they'd finished with her statement—she was very agitated and confused," he added, speaking rapidly.

"Were you there when . . ."

"When they removed the body?" James was struck throughout by the coldness of her tone and manner, but felt it must be shock.

"Yes, I stayed until the medical examiner came, until the forensics team came, and until they moved the body. There will have to be an—"

"An autopsy? Yes, I know, they phoned around noon." She looked at her watch. "Is it really only four o'clock. God." She sipped her brandy with closed eyes.

"Mrs. Darcy, is there someone I could phone, someone who could stay with you? I know this sounds presumptuous but . . ."

"No, it's all right. I've phoned my son. He's in California. Thank you for coming by to express your condolences," she said abruptly, as if dismissing him.

"Oh, that's not necessary. Actually I have another reason."

He thought she threw him a suspicious glance.

"I had been retained by Dr. Darcy to do some work for him which I would like to complete, despite or indeed because of this terrible outcome." James's voice thickened noticeably and he felt her icy stare.

"Don't tell me he hired you to follow me?" she asked sharply.

Startled, James spilled some of his drink onto his hand as he raised it to his lips. He put it down on the little decorative coaster she had provided.

"Pardon me?"

"Sorry. Go on," she added quickly.

"I assume you know that Dr. Darcy was having some problems, strange things happening around him . . ."

"I knew about the horse, yes, but I don't know what else you are referring to."

"Dr. Darcy asked me to investigate the horse's death, among other things. Now I am determined to investigate his murder."

"There's no need, Mr. Fleming. In fact, if it is money he owed you, I'm sure all that will be taken care of when the time comes." She paused. "He had his own lawyer of course."

James felt the words like a slap across his face. He wanted to know who this lawyer was.

"Mrs. Darcy, I assure you this is not about money. It is about honor and duty—and I might add, affection." James watched smugly as a red flush crept up her neck.

"Go on," she said at last.

"Do I have your permission to carry out your husband's wishes in this regard?" James persisted.

She glanced away.

"I have a very good relationship with the police, Mrs. Darcy." His implication was clear.

"All right," she said, adopting an offhand manner.

James pressed. "I'll take that as a yes."

"Yes, yes, go on."

"I would like to ask you about last night?"

"What about it?"

"Was Dr. Darcy in that position, on the desk, when you entered the office?" James, now rapidly developing a dislike for the woman, did not mince his words.

"No." She hesitated, overcome by some emotion, although James was unclear as to which.

He waited in silence.

"I knocked on his door, and when he didn't answer, I opened it. I was looking straight ahead, expecting to see him sitting at his desk. I expected, I think, to see him on the phone, since he hadn't called out to answer me."

"But you did expect to see him there?"

"Yes, I did. The waiting room was open and lit up, yes I assumed he was there."

"Go on, if you can." James was kinder now, remembering the horror of what he'd seen, aware of what she must have seen.

"As I said, I looked straight ahead. He was sitting in the chair and I thought—oh my God!" She shook her head, then took another, deeper sip of the brandy. "I couldn't say this before, to the police, to anyone, but I thought, I thought . . ." James could see she was having trouble getting the words out.

"Mrs. Darcy? What was it?"

"I thought he was laughing, somehow—grinning. His head was sort of back and I thought he was grinning but . . . it was the gaping . . . the gaping, oh, oh, I can't."

"It was the wound to his neck that you saw?" James was chilled to the bone as he tried to clarify what she was describing.

"Yes, I don't know if I screamed. Somehow I went over to him. Strange, I don't remember walking over to him. I went to touch him, but there was blood everywhere—on him, on his neck, his shirtfront, his lap. I don't know what happened next but I think I remember shoving him somehow."

"Shoving him?" James grew cold at her choice of words and he watched her even more closely.

"I couldn't stand it, the eyes, the thing across his neck, it was pumping. Aah . . . I pushed him forward and then he fell onto the desk. And that was worse. That sound, that awful sort of falling sound, a dead thump. I think I screamed then. I remember screaming and banging my back against the wall. There was someone in the room then."

"Mrs. Fogarty?"

"Yes. It must have been. After that things get very blurry."

"Of course, of course." He waited, nearly revolted at what she'd just described. She stood and refilled her glass without even glancing at him.

"Mrs. Darcy, if you don't mind . . . just one more thing, for now. When you drove into the car park, or when you were walking and entering the building, did you see anything or anybody? I mean see in the sense of noticing anything at all unusual."

"No, the police of course asked me that. No. I noticed the door of the other office, the cleaning ladies there, the sound of the hoovering. I know the medical staff who work there, but only slightly. Dr. Malone has a marvelous practice, an ophthalmologist—such a nice practice, prosperous, you know." She glanced up suddenly. "I would know them to speak to, but just casually. No one I knew was there and I walked on to Tom's office."

James noticed her manner toward him was changing.

"Do you know of anyone who would want to kill Dr. Darcy?" he asked quickly.

Joan Darcy was standing very still by the fireplace. Her expression began to harden and he heard impatience in her voice. He knew he was on sufferance now.

"Honestly, Mr. Fleming, I've answered all this for the police. If Tom had a patient crazy enough to do this I certainly wouldn't know about him. Or her." She put her brandy glass on the mantel. "And believe me, Tom, Dr. Darcy, would certainly not have broken confidentiality to tell me. Now, if that's all?" James stood up reluctantly, feeling he had only just begun.

She was seeing him to the door when the bell chimed in the hallway. Opening it, she smiled wanly at the good-looking man who was clearly startled to see James.

"I'm George Watson," he said affably, recovering from his surprise. "Are you from the police?"

"No, he's not, George, he was just leaving." And with that, James was summarily dismissed.

CHAPTER

—19—

GEORGE WATSON. GEORGE. WATSON. The two names echoed in James's brain as he drove out of the manicured cul-de-sac. He didn't know him by sight. But he knew that name.

Yes! Of course. One of the hotshot young real estate brokers who worked for Foy's.

He picked up the car phone and in seconds had Dave Whelan on the line.

"Standing by, boss. Mags told me all."

Mags, for heaven's sake, James said silently to himself.

"Right. What does the name George Watson mean to you?"

"You need to read the papers, James," Whelan retorted.

"Meaning?" James was sharpish.

"George Watson works for Foy's."

"Well, I knew that!" James swerved as an

oncoming car almost shaved him. One-hand driving—not good!

"And so did someone else."

"I imagine so."

"No, it was in the paper this morning. Mrs. Darcy. Joan, relict of the deceased. She too puts her fingers to the spindle at Foys and Co."

"No!"

"Yes."

"Do you know any, you know, any gossip?" James asked.

"Such as?" Whelan countered.

"Look, I just came from Mrs. Darcy. She said a strange thing to me when I said her husband had hired me. Before I could say why, she asked me if he'd hired me to follow her—"

"Ooh, that must have hurt."

"Shut up and listen. Darcy's dead, he was a prominent Dublin doctor. She's the daughter of a prominent Dublin doctor. The son's in California—"

"And is not a prominent doctor—"

"Point taken. Anyway. No one is there, at her house. No friends, no female relatives, as Jane Austen would say. No one. After this hideous loss. And then George Watson comes calling? If she thought Darcy wanted to have her followed—she must have had some guilty conscience?"

"I'm starting to see—"

"And Watson's that close to her—that he comes to her house? And she didn't introduce him to me."

"Smoke and fire?"

"I think so. Do the usual, right?"

"My pleasure, boss. This one is going to be good."

Whelan's endless enthusiasm for his job always buoyed James up, but once he was off the phone his depression fell like a curtain. He hesitated at the next set of lights, pondering where next to go.

Where else, but the scene of the crime.

James was fairly well known to the police force in Dublin and had no difficulty passing the yellow tape and entering the crime scene. In the car he'd formed a plan and now hoped to put it into action.

"I'd like the names of all the patients he saw yesterday," he said to Inspector Walsh, as they met in the corridor outside Darcy's office.

"Because your name is on there?" Walsh replied, sucking on the end of his ballpoint pen.

James was startled. He'd forgotten that.

"No, of course not."

"You think they're all suspects?"

"It's a place to start."

"So if you'd seen him earlier in the day, then you'd be one too?" Walsh smiled.

"Yes, I guess that's true. But I didn't, and you know I'm not. I found the body after two other people had found it."

"And I'm to believe you, that you came late to the scene? That's what both women also said."

"Yes, of course. You know you can believe me." But Walsh's slightly taunting question gave James pause. It was an assumption of his that because the two women seemed to have discovered the body that neither one was involved in the murder. He reflected on Mrs. Darcy's coldness and composure.

"I repeat, the patients he saw yesterday give us a place to start," James said at last, keeping his thoughts about Mrs. Darcy to himself.

"But what's to say it was a patient he'd seen Friday? Why not one he'd seen earlier in the week? Or a year ago?"

"Nothing." James shrugged.

"It's okay, James, I'm just a bit ahead of you. We're in the same boat. I'd be happy for your help on this one, especially since you knew the man. But I don't see how I can allow it."

"Yes, I knew him, professionally, on both sides of the desk. I'd seen him as a . . . doctor." James heard himself pause, self-conscious. "But he'd also retained me," he continued, "and I am still working under that professional agreement. In fact, the wife, the widow, just gave me verbal approval to continue."

"Quick young lad, aren't you?" Walsh said, scrutinizing James's face. "Tell me about it."

James quickly recounted the story of the death of Darcy's horse and that the report of it would be out at Stepaside police station. He mentioned also the scratches on the car, which seemed less important now than the letters Darcy had received. Walsh had called over one of his men to take down the details.

"Well this information does indeed give me a lead—thanks, Fleming. Tell me, what had you made of it all over these past weeks?"

James felt a flush of shame run through him. "Not a lot, I'm afraid."

"Did you at least figure it was all being done by one person?"

James started. "You know, Walsh, I made that assumption. But that's all it was. They needn't have been . . ."

Walsh started to walk away. "Listen, Fleming, you can look around, but don't remove anything from the crime scene."

"Right," said James as he stepped into the office where the officer in charge handed him a pair of surgical gloves. Carefully, James searched Darcy's desk, and easily found his appointment calendar. He wrote down the names of the clients for that Friday and then jotted down the names for the week.

He groaned inwardly; there were twenty-eight in all. This would be a job for the police after all, he felt. He didn't have the resources to do such massive interviewing. He stood up from the desk, straightening his back. He'd been standing because the police had already removed the chair Darcy had been sitting in—not that he would have sat in it, he thought with a shudder.

His initial thought was that something had unhinged one of the patients—possibly on that Friday—and that the patient had reacted out of sudden powerful feelings, not feelings that had simmered for days or weeks. But that theory was belied by the killing of Quixote—assuming the two killings were related. Remembering the date of his first meeting with Darcy at the police station, he flipped the calendar to the date before that, to the Thursday the horse had been killed, and quickly copied down the names of the patients. Some names happened to be the same, some were different. Oh, that would be too easy, James said to himself as he compared them. He glanced around, spotting the long low filing cabinet. He'd pull the records on those patients at least. But he stopped when he saw the seals across the drawers and went instead to find Walsh.

"I just want a quick look at the files on the patients," he said ingenuously.

Walsh again smiled his slow knowing smile. "Look, Fleming, you might be in real estate, but you know better. Those files are confidential. I'm not even sure where I stand on those. In fact I'm awaiting a ruling. And if I need a ruling, you certainly would. Patients' medical files? Come on!"

"But the answer will be in there."

"Then if it is, I'll find it. I've got a call in to the department as we speak. If I get the go-ahead, I'll start reading them tonight. I agree, there'll be clues there, but not for your eyes."

James wandered back to the office which, with the ongoing removal of items from the scene, was becoming increasingly denuded. It felt eerie and he wanted to get out of there. He was alone since the men were now negotiating the heavy file down the narrow corridor—the file that held all the clues as far as James was concerned. He was convinced he would recognize the murderer from Darcy's notes, even if Darcy himself had not.

The phone stood stark and alone on the stained desktop. It was, he knew, a companion to the one on Mrs. Fogarty's desk. Quickly he took out his own handheld tape recorder and pressed the Record button. Then, holding his breath, he pressed Replay on Darcy's phone and let the one tape play very softly onto the other as he watched the door. He didn't know whether any of this was confidential, but he wasn't going to ask, and he didn't want to be caught. He'd played it so softly he wasn't able to listen. Thrilled with his piece of detective work he pocketed the recorder and pulled off the gloves.

Glancing around for what he knew would be the last time, he heaved a sigh and walked quickly from the office to gasp the fresh air outside. Putting his excitement and curiosity on hold he drove directly to Mrs. Fogarty's house.

"Mrs. Fogarty, I am so glad you're able to see me today at such short notice."

Mrs. Fogarty was very pale and her eyes and nose were red from crying.

"I'm happy to help, Mr. Fleming," she said as she poured out the tea and waved her children away to their rooms.

"I told the police what I know." She glanced at her watch. "It's just over twenty-four hours since . . ."

"I know," James said sadly. It was late Saturday afternoon but the day had taken on that timeless quality reserved to days of tragedy and loss. Unless he did a check, he too would lose track of the day and the hour.

"The police have a lot of the real journeyman work to do, Mrs. Fogarty."

"Please call me Anne."

James explained how Dr. Darcy had engaged him to work on finding Quixote's killer, and how he now was actively working on finding Darcy's murderer, with Mrs. Darcy's agreement.

"In a way I have more flexibility than the police, Anne, and I can get started straight away if you can help me."

"By all means. I want to help," she said eagerly, spooning sugar into her tea.

James explained that he needed to have some sense of the patients on the list he had in his notebook. He was hoping to eliminate some of the twenty-eight people that had been seen at the office that week, in fact a lot of them if possible. Mrs. Fogarty explained, as she studied the list, that she knew most of them by name and sight, and some from having typed Darcy's notes.

Quickly she went down the list, and as she talked, James was impressed at how professional she was, how detailed in her observations and astute in her judgments, and he said so.

"Surprised at a housewife like me?" she said with a smirk.

"I didn't mean it that way—"

"Sure you did, but it's all right."

James took another cup of tea.

"I loved my job, I loved the patients. And of course I loved Dr. Darcy. I started out in nursing

but never finished. Got married, like a fool." She
grimaced. "I'd always wanted to help people. In
helping Dr. Darcy that filled a need for me. It
wasn't just being a secretary. I took an interest.
And in a funny way I felt good when I saw the
results he would get with his patients—either
those on meds or those that came for therapy."

She explained to James that some of the names
on his list were long-term patients of Dr. Darcy's
who came in on a very fixed schedule with their
blood test results and to have their medications
adjusted or renewed. James was convinced by her
knowledgeable manner that he could put them at
the bottom of the list, if not—which he was
inclined to do—eliminate them altogether.

Of the remaining eighteen Mrs. Fogarty herself
eliminated nearly ten. James queried her certainty.

"Mr. Fleming, I tell you these patients are by
and large elderly people."

"Elderly?"

"Yes, I don't know how much you know about
therapy and such, but the elderly—they often suf-
fer from depression."

"That may be." This thought had never struck
James and he felt ignorant. "But in Ireland—
going to a psychiatrist?"

"Well I should tell you some of these people
are well-heeled, very educated kind of people
who would be open to the idea of getting help.
Some of them though were sent by their GPs.
Probably didn't know what to do with them.
Trust me, Mr. Fleming, at least out of this list,
there are maybe ten who would be young enough

and strong enough to kill poor Dr. Darcy—" Mrs. Fogarty suddenly sobbed and James too was moved.

"You feel able to go on?"

"Certainly." She sighed. "I feel this is the least I can do. I don't mind telling you, Mr. Fleming, because I can see how much you liked the doctor—I loved him in my own way, and I can't believe he's gone."

James was silent again. Clearly Mrs. Fogarty had loved Darcy, perhaps more than as a friend. He looked at her as though for the first time. She was, despite her tear-streaked face, not unattractive. She had a good figure although a little plump, thick chestnut hair, her blue eyes could be merry and flirtatious perhaps. Warm, affectionate, sincere—the opposite of Joan Darcy?

As though reading his mind, Anne spoke seriously. "I did say in my own way, Mr. Fleming. He was married and so was I." She looked around at the plain sitting room as if saying this was her life. "I had a little fantasy."

"Who doesn't?" James replied kindly.

"Such a lovely personality. I suspected Mrs. Darcy didn't appreciate him or his work. She'd come into the office. She was always a bit aloof, arrogant I suppose. She has that awfully plummy, convent school accent. Loretto, I used to say to myself. They seemed to turn them out for years. I'm being petty now, I'm sorry. He had a way with him, didn't he, Mr. Fleming?"

"Yes, indeed he did."

"People could be drawn to him. I always

thought it was his eyes. They were soft and wise, so understanding without saying a word, you know?"

James nodded.

"And he was very attractive to women."

"He was?"

"Oh yes. All the women patients were half in love with him themselves." She smiled wanly. "I was one of a crowd. But apparently it happens."

"In therapy?"

"Mm."

James reflected that it happened to men as well, but he didn't say this aloud.

"Anne, this gives me an idea. Would any one of these patients, do you think, have loved him and felt spurned by him perhaps?" He was searching for the right words.

"Well, I worked for him for five years, and if you're really asking did he have an affair or sleep with a patient, I would say no. He was a very ethical man. But I could see, oh I hate to say this, but he seemed to have a favorite here and there. He'd take that bit more interest, or look a little brighter, there'd be a difference somehow. I suppose because I felt that way about him, I would notice."

"Do you think Mrs. Darcy did?"

"I don't know. I think there was trouble there but I don't know what it was. My guess, though, is that she wasn't happy with him being a therapist. Her father is Mr. Thompson, a very big consultant and surgeon. She has a brother, a doctor in England, and one in the States. Very, very successful. A real medical family. I don't think she felt she got what she wanted—that kind of social life and prominence. She strikes me as being ashamed of Dr. Darcy."

"Or disappointed?"

"Yes, that's the word. Silly woman. Anyway, couldn't she have been a doctor herself, if she chose? Why live through him?" Her voice was angry. She looked up at the sounds of her children squabbling in the kitchen. "God, it's tea time and I have nothing in."

James, suddenly aware of how tired they both were, focused their attention on the list. Mentally he had taken Mrs. Fogarty off his own. If Walsh went that route he was crazy. This woman was as solid as rock.

By the time James left, he had a shorter list: he looked at the names and wondered how on earth he could approach them. More to the point, he wondered if one of them was the name of the murderer. He saw in flashback the gaping wound in Tom's neck and shivered. As he got in his Citröen and turned on the ignition, waiting for the car to rise in its characteristically unique way, he sagged against the seat. God, how he would love to go for a pint with Matt. Matt, wise, sensible, practical Matt—so far away in Australia. He wanted to sit down in a pub and drink and talk through his ideas about the case. He thought of Geraldine, but turned his car for home.

CHAPTER
——— 20 ———

ACTUALLY, A FULL night's sleep without benefit of pints had done James a world of good and he was fresh and alert early on Sunday morning. As he pottered around making coffee and throwing his wash into the washing machine, he consciously replaced the sadness he felt over Darcy with the single goal of finding his killer.

It occurred to him as he studied the list over his breakfast that neither he nor Mrs. Fogarty had shown any scruples at all. He had asked her what she knew about each of the patients, and she had willingly told him all that she knew or speculated or could remember from the files. He wondered if Darcy had had any idea that the closely guarded files now in police hands were in a different form in Mrs. Fogarty's memory.

He looked over the notes beside each name. Where to begin?

Elizabeth, he now knew, was already a mur-

derer—of sorts. She seemed an obvious suspect.
She had killed before, and with a knife. And of all
the people on this list at least, she was an invol-
untary patient—seeing Darcy not by choice but
by court mandate. She could have resented that.
But was that a motive?

Emily. Mrs. Fogarty had indicated that she
thought Emily had a bit of a crush on Darcy, and
that the doctor had seemed to her to have a soft
spot for Emily. If anything, such a situation, if
known, would go toward Mrs. Darcy's motiva-
tion, not Emily's, James believed. Mrs. Fogarty
had described her as tall, but in appearance
almost delicate. Could she have killed a horse?
Could she have sliced open a man's neck? James
put her name at the end, but he knew why. Her
persona was haunting him because—even now—
another woman, an academic too, was languish-
ing in prison because of a case that he had
solved. Of course Emily was a possibility, James
sighed, but one he didn't want to face straight-on.

Mary Kealy seemed out of the question since,
according to Mrs. Fogarty, she was so depressed
she could hardly move. But her husband, Brian,
had potential. James now knew that he was angry
with Darcy for not curing his wife. He was young,
big, and strong, as Anne had described him. But
surely this kind of personality would confront
Darcy head-on, beat him to a pulp perhaps, but
not creep around a stable to find Darcy's horse?

Mr. Edwards had seemed fairly ordinary to
Mrs. Fogarty. But what she had remembered
about him was that he was divorced. There still

weren't many divorced people in Ireland and she had never met one. She felt sorry for him. A fine-looking man. A businessman. James himself had no feeling one way or the other about him.

This Mullins character struck James, however. Mrs. Fogarty had said he was a bit odd. "Uptight" had been her word. He was a big man. James nearly scoffed at himself. Now a man was a murder suspect because he was big and uptight! James realized he was drawn to the men on the list merely because they were men. James shook head, annoyed with himself, and read through the list again, this time without bias. Either a man or a woman could wield a knife behind an unsuspecting victim's back. That was it!

James glanced at the clock and quickly dialed Walsh's number. Of course it didn't pick up. In a hurry now, he thought of the medical examiner. He dialed his number and left a message. Within minutes Dr. Harrison returned the call.

"An ordinary carving knife, Fleming. Common to a thousand homes. Very sharp however, probably new."

"You have the weapon?"

"No, but I can tell, Fleming, from the wound—"

"Enough. I'll take your word for it."

"Ten inches. As I said, very common."

James felt chilled after he spoke with Harrison, and he stood for a while watching out his sitting room window. The day was gray, drizzling and bleak. The leaves that had clung on to the trees had finally been stripped away by Saturday night's driving rain. His energetic mood had evaporated and now the loneliness of the night before crept back in. He thought again of Matt, picturing him in some sun-baked spot, barbecuing something, his children sprawled around him and his loving wife mixing up some kind of fruity punch. He looked again at the rain zigging and zagging down his window and thought of Geraldine. Clearly she hadn't thought of him—his tape was blank when he'd returned and the phone hadn't rung since. He thought of going into his office on Monday and his stomach churned. There was work overdue, waiting for him, but he had no taste for any of it now.

He thought of his brother, Donald, eligible bachelor doctor, and his endless invitations for long weekends in country houses. He thought of his mother, no doubt having sherry with her numerous friends on her cul-de-sac, Mack munching something quite unsuitable and resting at her feet.

He thought back to his childhood. Sunday morning had once been so ordered for him. Get up, have breakfast; the four of them, off to church, when he was older teach a junior Sunday school class. Back home to wait for Sunday dinner, a roast joint of some sort, and roast potatoes, apple tart afterward. He and Donald would kick the soccer ball around the back garden, a nap by the fire, a little homework for school the next day. Where had it all gone? Could he recapture it? Did he want to? Had he been happy? Had they? Were Whelan and his wife happy, or Mrs. Fogarty and her husband? Darcy and his wife—

had they been happy once? Maggie and her current boyfriend?

James turned from the window: he suddenly saw he had no choices. This was the task in hand—to find poor Darcy's killer.

The carving knife could be in anybody's kitchen. Even as he walked downstairs to the car park James had no sense of where to start. As he unlocked his car, he saw his tape recorder on the seat.

"God, what a fool!" he said aloud as he got in and locked the doors. Excitedly he pressed the Play button and turned the volume full up. Yes! It had worked. These were the calls that had been left on Darcy's tape.

The first call was from a patient not on James's list. A man's voice identifying himself and asking for some clarification about his health insurance claim and to verify the dates he'd seen Darcy the year before. James quickly eliminated him. The next call was from Edwards. He too identified himself and said: "Darcy, I'm returning your call, although I have nothing to say except that you are never to call me at my home or office again. I am terminating treatment and your bill will be paid in full."

James was caught by the very caustic tone of the man's voice. The anger there forced James to put Edwards on his short list. The next call was a pharmaceutical representative. Nothing of interest there. The call that followed was from a woman—James cursed, she didn't identify herself—but she said she was confirming her appointment for that afternoon, Friday. James looked at his list of the appointments. She must have been a regular, thought James, if she thought Darcy would know her voice. Or perhaps she was just addled or embarrassed at using a tape, as some people did become.

The last call, as it turned out, was from Joan Darcy. She wasn't a happy caller either—she sounded demanding, even cold. But this corroborated what Mrs. Fogarty had told him about Joan's call to her. Apparently Tom Darcy had arranged to meet his wife at six o'clock that Friday night and she was furious that he was late.

To have been so angry at him for being late and probably at that very point he was either dead or dying—what regret she must be feeling. Or else! The thought struck James—perhaps Joan Darcy had been setting up her own alibi? She needn't have been calling from home. And it was she, after all, who had found the body. That made a horrible kind of logic. As his wife, she would be the first to be expected to have noticed he was late or missing from home. Why not hasten the process by phoning Tom's tape, by then phoning the ever loyal Mrs. Fogarty, by returning to the office and be found discovering Tom's body? She would know the routine of the other occupants of the building, a place that would be virtually empty late on a Friday afternoon. Mrs. Fogarty would be coming right along behind her—to witness the grieving distraught widow? The widow finding the body would garner sympathy, not suspicion. James shivered despite the efficient heat of his car.

James had already half decided to start with Edwards in order to eliminate him, but having heard the tape he was determined to see this man and learn what he could about why he was so angry, or at least so rude to Tom. Edwards first, he decided. And then in whatever order he could see them he would approach Mullins, Emily, Elizabeth, perhaps Mary. And then there's Joan Darcy! he murmured to himself as he turned out onto the street heading for the affluent village of Foxrock where Edwards lived. Yes—there was always Joan.

As James approached Edwards's home he realized that the lovely detached house with its beautifully manicured grounds confirmed what he had learned after a couple of discreet calls to lawyer friends. Edwards was a successful, fairly low profile businessman who sat on the boards of a few cultural organizations. Little else was known about him.

The gate to the drive was closed, and James pulled the car up on the pavement of the narrow street and walked toward the garden gate. He was relieved to see what he assumed to be Edwards's car parked on the gravel. Behind it, in the garage, he could see another car, and this alarmed him. If Edwards had company he'd never talk to him, and James wanted to get this over as quickly as possible. With some trepidation he rang the bell.

James immediately introduced himself to the

man who opened the door as a solicitor working on the Darcy murder case. He watched as Edwards's face closed over. He stepped outside, pulling the door behind him.

"How dare you come to my house on a Sunday," Edwards hissed, and James took a step back in astonishment.

"I'm interviewing as many people as possible about this case, Mr. Edwards. I knew you were a patient, a current patient. I also know that you telephoned Dr. Darcy on the day of his death— one of the few people who did." James brazened it out as Edwards stared at him, his eyes bulging with anger.

Edwards seemed suddenly to make a decision. His face relaxed, and glancing around as if to see if his neighbors had observed him, he asked James to follow him. They stepped into the house and he led James into a small study, or rather a morning room off the front foyer. Indicating a chair, he stepped back into the foyer and crossed to another room that James took to be the sitting room, and spoke through the open door.

"Sorry, Mother. A small matter of business. I won't be long." James heard him shut the sitting room door and quickly took his seat, looking around at the fine leather-bound books on the shelves and the deep leather chairs, and the thick Persian rug on the floor. Oh, money, real money, he sighed.

Edwards shut the door with a bang and strode to a chair; sitting on the edge, he began without preamble.

"I want to know exactly what you know about me and how you know it."

"Why?" James countered.

Startled, Edwards paused. "For this single reason. I was told by Darcy himself that our work together was confidential. Of course, I saw in the papers that he was murdered, and of course I was sorry. I was concluding my relationship with him anyway. My point is, what exactly is the meaning of the word confidential when you can arrive here, knowing my name, my address, and that I was a patient? I want to know what you know about me." James noted an edge on the last word. Edwards had clasped his hands loosely in front of him, and James knew he was barely holding himself in. He decided to be truthful.

"Mr. Edwards, I know only what I just told you. I know that from his desk calendar and the telephone book."

"And that I phoned?"

James grimaced. "I played the tape."

"That's all?"

"Yes." James realized this was all going to be even harder than he thought.

"Didn't Darcy keep notes?"

"Yes."

"Where are they?"

"The police have them."

Edwards was expressionless and silent.

"May I ask you why you were finishing with Dr. Darcy?" James asked finally.

"I had trouble sleeping. He'd prescribed some medication. Things had run their course. Now, if

that is all." He said this with finality and started
to stand.

"Your voice on the tape sounded very angry,
Mr. Edwards. It occurs to me that you were on
the verge of losing your temper with Dr. Darcy a
mere two or three hours before his death." He
watched as Edwards sat down.

"It also occurs to me that if you were finishing
up, as with a medical doctor as you suggest,
there would have been no need for such rage,
such rudeness. Would there?"

"Are you saying I am a suspect?"

"Well as they say, everyone's a suspect at the
beginning. Darcy's wife, his secretary, his patients,
you—" James knew his tone was taunting.

The man reacted. "This is outrageous! I think
we're finished here, Fleming."

Edwards stood up and yanked open the door
of the study. Stepping into the hall with James
behind him, he was clearly startled to see the
woman standing there. Covering his confusion
he introduced James to his mother, Mrs.
Edwards.

James was surprised. He guessed she must be
in her early sixties, but she looked years younger.
A tall woman with dark, beautifully arranged
hair, large dark eyes, a striking, rather sultry col-
oring. She was certainly five foot ten and quite
erect. Clearly very fit. She shook hands with
James and he felt, as her eyes swept over his suit,
his hair, that he was being assessed.

"I love to meet Martin's friends."

"Well, business acquaintance, actually," said

Edwards, his demeanor now seemingly warmer toward James as he edged toward the front door.

"Oh, but that's how so many friendships begin, Martin. James Fleming. Do I know that name?"

James cringed inwardly. It had occurred to him that Mrs. Edwards might move in some circles that would overlap his mother's social circles. He knew that she was assuming, rightly so, that Fleming was a Protestant name.

"My brother is a physician," he said lamely.

"How nice, but I think it is your mother I have met. She supports the opera, does she not?"

"Yes, she's very fond of music." James was succinct to the point of rudeness.

"That's it then. And wasn't there some connection with the violinist Sarah Gallagher? How is she?"

"She's on tour, in America." James was now as impatient as Edwards that he get to the front door.

"Tell your mother that I send greetings. If you are to be a regular here, we might arrange to have coffee one morning, or afternoon tea. You and your mother?"

"I'll mention it," James said hastily as he made his escape.

Back in his car he reviewed the events. Edwards was far too angry and nervous about the confidentiality issue to be concerned merely about what sleeping pills Darcy might have noted in his record. There had to be more. He was divorced, but that would not account for the anger—the divorce would be a matter of public record. James suspected that Edwards had a secret and now was very afraid it was in the files, there for Walsh at least to see—whenever he got to them.

James thought of the scenario: Edwards had confided in Tom, then he regretted it. He decided to break off the therapy and he phoned. Perhaps Tom had phoned him back. Something unhinged Edwards and he went to the office. It had to be premeditated, because whoever did it had to bring the knife.

In killing Darcy, Edwards would have thought the secret, whatever it was, would die with him. Now he realized it might exist somewhere else. But there was no way Edwards could get to those files now.

James cursed himself. If he hadn't been so open with Edwards about the location of the files, he might have laid a trap for him. Too late now. He'd have to do more legwork regarding Edwards.

"Whelan," he said into his car phone.

Whelan had little to report on Watson's dalliance with Mrs. Darcy. He'd gone to one showing of a house and engaged a young female broker from Foy's in conversation, but he had learned nothing. But he was working the phones and felt optimistic.

"Okay, Dave. Keep up the hard work and a log of your hours, right? I also want you to find out what you can about Martin Edwards, and see if you can get me the name and address of the woman who was married to him, and later divorced. Also, get me the number of Professor

Emily Lawlor. I think I want to see her as soon as possible."

As James passed a small local hotel he knew well, he decided to stop in and treat himself to Sunday lunch. He loved these traditional meals: good sliced roast beef with a touch of crackly fat, a tasty pan gravy, delicious boiled potatoes. The peas were mushy and the broccoli was limp, but with that gravy it was all like heaven. Comfort food, he thought, as he patted his belly, and then dipped into the apple tart and cream and finished off with a strong cup of coffee. Whelan had got back to him, and as James emerged into the watery sunlight he felt like a man new made. It was time to head for Trinity and get one more interview out of the way before he faced the difficult Monday that lay ahead of him.

CHAPTER

—— 21 ——

AS JAMES SPRINTED through Back Gate at Trinity College and past the playing fields, he was flooded with memories of his own college days. But his age caught up with him as he had to stop to draw breath before entering the ancient building known as the Rubrics.

He quickly found Emily Lawlor's set of rooms on the ground floor, and tapped gently on the low door.

"Professor Lawlor?" he said, surprise in his voice as he saw the young slender woman in front of him.

"Yes, Mr. Fleming? Do come in."

James sat in the low chair she indicated and she stirred the small fire in the tiny grate.

"Don't tell anyone," she whispered conspiratorially. "There isn't quite a ban on these fires, but the college doesn't approve. But I love a real fire on these autumn days. I needed to get caught up on reading my students' essays and love doing it here."

"This reminds me of my tutor's rooms, years ago. He too would have a fire in the grate. There was no problem with it then." James stopped, conscious of his age yet again, and he looked more carefully at the woman as she sat at her desk.

She reminded him in some way—perhaps her hair, or her intensity, or the seriousness of her expression—of Brona. Shivers passed through him as he wondered briefly at what her life was like now in prison, where he had worked so hard to put her. He was on the point of asking if Miss Lawlor had known that other doctoral student, but instantly thought the better of that faux pas.

"I appreciate your seeing me, Professor."

"Oh, please call me Emily. 'Professor' makes me uncomfortable." James noticed her self-deprecation.

"But you are, are you not?"

"Well, for a three-year appointment. I hope it works out, I have another year here. I do so want to prove myself."

Again James was struck by her lack of confidence. He tried to imagine her cutting the throat of a horse, and so he persevered.

"What is your specialty then?"

"Coleridge," she said, brightening.

"Ah, the sea of faith and all that."

"Well, I touch on the poetry, but I concentrate on the prose that followed on his poetic period."

"Do you deal with his opium addiction?"

James was almost dismissive, although he'd studied the great Romantic poets himself.

Professor Lawlor stiffened her back. "I deal with it of course; and sympathetically if you'd like genuinely to know. My theory has been that Coleridge suffered from manic-depression. Great periods of wild productivity, followed by terrible depressions. I do believe he was using brandy and opium to self-medicate." She was nearly out of breath, but James saw the fire beneath her demeanor and wished he could ask her directly why she had been a patient of Dr. Darcy. Did she too have wild mood swings that he couldn't detect right now? Although slim, she was tall and strong, and had a very firm handshake. Could she have slit a horse's throat, or a man's when he was not expecting someone to come up behind him?

"Do you ride, Professor, I mean, Emily?"

"Pardon?"

"Do you ride, horses, or have you ever?"

"What has this to do with Dr. Darcy's death?" James had underestimated her.

"Darcy rode."

"Yes?"

"You had an appointment with him his last day at the office?"

"Friday, that is correct."

"Did you notice anything or anyone—anything that now, in retrospect, might strike you as significant to the investigation?"

"No, Mr. Fleming, there was no one in the waiting room. I don't think I ever saw a patient waiting. Perhaps coming out of the door, but not waiting. Dr. Darcy never ran over." She said this proudly, possessively, and it struck a chord with James.

"Do you mind telling me how long you'd been seeing him?"

"Two years, since I began this job, this post I should say. He was very helpful."

James watched helplessly as she lowered her head and slow tears began to run down her face.

"I saw it in the paper. I picked up the morning paper and there it was, on the front page. I was standing in the street, Grafton Street, on my way here to do a little reading. People were walking past me and I couldn't move. I wanted to cry out but there was no one." She looked up at him frankly. "You can't know what it's like. Your therapist dies, is murdered! Who are you going to share that with? No one. And yet I grieve. I've thought of going to the funeral, but I know I couldn't. It would be such an intrusion."

She stood up, occupying herself with the fire yet again, a way to deflect attention from herself, he realized. James too stood up.

She turned, crying still. "Just like that. Gone. I needed him. He helped me. I thought I loved him, but in these few days I realize it wasn't that kind of romantic love I thought it was. I had gotten carried away. But I respected him. He was a fine, good man. I loved all that goodness in him. And I have no one to tell, no one to cry with."

"Yes, you do," said James softly.

Emily Lawlor looked at him intently.

"Yes?" she said softly. "You too?"

"Yes," James whispered and moved closer to her. Hesitating briefly, she moved toward him, and they held each other in a close embrace that within seconds became more than mutual support as their lips met and they kissed deeply.

James and Emily pulled apart as suddenly as they'd come together.

"I'm terribly sorry," James said hastily.

"No, no. I don't know. It is I who am sorry."

There was an awkward silence that James broke.

"I know what happened. At least on my part." He sat down again near the fire, not looking at Emily.

"Yes," she answered.

"It was when you were speaking of Darcy just now. You were putting into words how I felt. It overwhelmed me that I could share with someone else the feelings I am having. I knew him. You knew him. I think we, or at least I, needed him in my life. He was helping me move on. It just feels so good to know someone else feels that. Oh, God, that sounds so selfish as I say the words aloud."

"No, it doesn't," Emily replied, sitting near him now. "I felt, I feel the same. Listen, James. I am not dense. I know you came here initially to question me. Somewhere in your mind you were thinking I could be a suspect in Dr. Darcy's murder. I hope you know without my putting it into words—but I will put it into words. I learned from him the importance of speaking directly. I am telling you, I didn't kill him. I want you to believe that."

"Yes," James answered, directly also. "Yes, I know you couldn't have done it! I feel it and I believe you."

James stood up abruptly.

"I have a lot to do on this, Emily. I should be going."

"Of course," she said, a small sad smile passing across her face. "But perhaps you could let me know the outcome of your search for the killer?"

James did not answer at first. "You know, I am going to the funeral. We could go together." He let the question hang in the air.

"No, I still believe I would be an intruder. I was not a part of his personal life. Much as I fantasized about it, I know the boundaries." She straightened her shoulders as she said it. "His loss is a terrible one for me, but I know I can go on. Because he taught me how." Tears welled in her eyes.

"But it would be good to speak of it occasionally, wouldn't it?"

"Yes," she said softly. "I'd like that. Very much."

CHAPTER
—— 22 ——

THE NEXT DAY passed in a blur for James. He'd spent the day at his desk, catching up on the work he had let slide. Maggie and his associates all had their shoulders to the wheel and also, he noticed, had kept out of his way because his mood was so gloomy. The only bright spot, he said to himself ironically, was Whelan's visit. He had a "load of gossip," as he described it.

As he recounted to James, Mrs. Darcy had been rather flirtatious in her three years at Foy's. All of the co-workers had commented on it, surprised at first. She flirted with the buyers. She flirted with the vendors. She did good steady work, however, earned excellent commissions, and Foy's were happy with her productivity so no one ever said anything. Finally, the staff got used to it, particularly after they'd met Darcy. He wasn't any fun, as they said, and he'd made people uncomfortable. They thought he was analyzing them. No one was really very surprised or even interested when she started in on George, the flirting between them was mutual and, they thought, harmless, until they were observed kissing and touching. There was a lot of body language and less of the flirting. The word around Foy's was they were sleeping together, or, if not, they soon would. No one seemed to care. Whelan was disgusted

"People should care."

"Why?" James asked as he handed Whelan a cup of coffee.

"Because it would have put a brake on their behavior, having an affair for godsakes."

James smiled to himself. Whelan was an odd mix. He was a hard chaw that had seen the raw side of life and yet he was easily shocked and could be very straightlaced. In this instance James found himself agreeing with him. He felt sad, so sorry for Darcy. Did he know he was being cuckolded? Had they discussed divorce? He asked Whelan what he knew.

"Oh, well, I know nothing. But the gossip was that Mrs. Darcy was pretty excited when the divorce bill went through, and staff assumed it wasn't because of her feminist political philosophy."

"Do you think you can talk to Watson?"

"I've been wrestling with that. I'm not sure how. I've tailed him in my free time and he spent all of yesterday with Mrs. Darcy."

"Oh God," James groaned. "It looks like this is something I'll need to address. If Darcy wouldn't willingly give Joan a divorce, that could make Joan or Watson or both, people with a real motive."

"Oh, come on," Whelan scoffed.

"Why the hell not?"

"She could have just left him and lived with whoever."

"Maybe she isn't that kind? She comes from a prominent family."

"Oh, so she'd kill her husband rather than just go off and live with someone openly." Whelan was sarcastic. "Fleming, which is worse?"

"Then maybe she hated him. Just hated him. And it built and it was a crime of passion—in reverse." James faltered. "Okay, we'll leave them for the moment. I think Edwards has something to hide too."

"Why?"

James recounted Edwards's obsessive concern with the files.

Whelan was pragmatic. "Look, from what you say, a man that successful in business would immediately think in terms of reports, notes, files, memoranda."

"So what are you saying?"

"That his so-called fear is not enough. He's just a crazy guy, concerned with his privacy. Look, if he did kill Darcy, he would have killed him and taken the files."

"But nothing was disturbed. I was there, remember?"

Whelan shrugged. "All he had to do was open the cabinet, remove his file, close the cabinet."

"But that itself would point the finger at him!" James exclaimed. "He'd have to have taken more than his own to throw off suspicion."

Whelan shrugged. "Well, I'll keep an open mind. Are you going to the funeral tomorrow?"

"Yes, of course. You know, Whelan, I knew Darcy and I liked him. But I'd go anyway. I've got a plan. I'll tackle Watson and Mrs. Darcy. Meanwhile, I'd like you to dig into Elizabeth's background." James gave Whelan the necessary information to go on with and watched as he limped away.

CHAPTER
——— 2 3 ———

THE FUNERAL WAS, as James expected, very well attended. It seemed that at least half of Dublin's medical community was there, and James even spotted his brother, Donald. It was a wet and windy morning and people rushed from their cars to the church, giving James no chance to linger or talk or observe. As the Mass wore on he tuned out the homily, the brief eulogy, and sat in a daze while the hundreds of mourners went to take Communion. He was so far back he could not see Joan Darcy or who was sitting with her in the front pew, but he did see Mrs. Fogarty kneeling near one of the columns, her rosary beads pressed to her forehead as she bent in prayer and grief.

As the coffin started up the aisle and the organ played the recessional, James had difficulty restraining his own tears, and he wished he were anywhere at that moment than where he was.

At the cemetery it was much the same,

although fewer people had braved the rain. He still was kept to the far fringes of the crowd, and he turned, disheartened, to find his car and trail the others slowly out of the cemetery. Neither the Mass nor the graveside service had given him any sense of consolation, nor any feeling of peace and acceptance. Darcy was dead and he shouldn't be. It was as simple as that.

James kept the funeral cars in sight, and guessing the wake would not be at Darcy's home, followed the line of cars to a well-known hotel on Dublin's south side.

The room was large and warm where the guests assembled and the drinks were plentiful. James ordered a large whiskey and meandered around the room, looking for Watson and hoping Donald had stayed away.

Finally spotting Watson with what looked like a crowd of staff from Foy's whom he knew by sight, James worked his way over beside him and got his attention. They turned off into one of the small side rooms. Watson looked both grave and puzzled.

"I've met you before," he said.

"Yes, I am investigating Darcy's murder. This might seem tactless, but I need to know, if only to eliminate you both, if you and Mrs. Darcy were, let me say, hoping to marry?"

James was unnerved, as Watson merely looked at him in astonishment.

"Let me put it this way—do you know if Mrs. Darcy had asked Darcy for a divorce?"

"This is a funeral, Fleming."

"Yes, I know that, of a murdered man, a man I knew and liked. I can ask you, or I can ask Mrs. Darcy."

"I think you had better leave."

"That's not for you to determine, Watson. I'm not making a scene. Just answer the question—or shall I take your not answering as sufficient?"

"Of course I didn't kill Darcy. Of course Joan didn't either. We're close, yes. But we're not talking about marriage. I'm not certainly. She's ten years older, Fleming!" He said this to James as if it explained everything.

James persisted. "Do you know or suspect that she discussed a divorce with Darcy?"

"She might have mentioned something about that."

"And?"

"That's all I know. Now you must excuse me. I'm leaving if you're not."

James shrugged and Watson did as good as his word, and left.

James hesitated. Reserved by nature and polite by training, he disliked intensely this part of his work. But he dreaded postponing it too. For the next half hour he observed Joan Darcy, surrounded at all times by people offering their condolences, and he realized that it was not realistic to attempt to confront her there. Leaving the wake he filled the intervening hours with a visit to Edwards's former wife.

James found Mrs. Edwards's neat little house on a steep coastal road that had a partial view of

Dalkey harbor. It was white stone with deep-set windows. Absolutely gorgeous, thought James, and realized that he was sick to death of his flat, no more so than now.

He rang the bell. The door was quickly opened by a woman in her forties, dressed in an artist's smock with paint smudges on her hands, on her small pale face, and even in her hair. She listened intently as James explained who he was, and how he hoped she would feel able to talk to him about her former husband.

Lost in thought, she led James to a small sunny sitting room, sparsely but prettily furnished with pieces in bright primary colors.

"You honestly are suggesting that Martin could kill someone, this Dr. Darcy?"

"Dr. Darcy was a psychiatrist and—"

"Oh, how interesting." She suddenly seemed engaged, and James relaxed as he talked.

"Mr. Edwards was ending his relationship with Darcy. He didn't elaborate with me. But I heard his voice on a tape and he sounded very angry, too angry for what he described as a simple professional relationship that involved no more than a prescription for sleeping pills."

"Martin always had trouble sleeping, Mr. Fleming."

"But he was still angry when I talked to him and, I think, very worried about the fact that Darcy's files are in police hands."

"I am surprised by this. You see, Mr. Fleming, the Martin I knew was very controlled; he rarely showed any emotion. So in that sense I would agree that for him to be angry and show it might indicate something—but not that he could act on that anger and—kill! He is not a killer, Mr. Fleming. If anything, I would have said he was too passive." She looked down at her hands, and realizing they were a startling mix of yellow and green, she rubbed at them with her smock.

"You must excuse my appearance," she said simply.

"Well, clearly you're an artist," said James, smiling back. "May I see your work?"

"Yes, you may." She smiled and led him to a sunny little room she'd converted to a studio. Some of her paintings were quite nice, he thought. Small seascapes, and scenes of Dalkey— the cliffs, the coastline and the village. They had a charm, a sweetness, that he thought must come from her own personality.

"How is it that you are divorced, Ms. Edwards?" He asked suddenly.

"That was Martin's doing, I'm afraid. I loved him; I still do. I kept his name, as you must realize."

"Yes."

"It was never a passionate love. I admired him and his steadfastness. He's good at his work. He likes the things I like, a little classical music, art, a little travel. Fine food and wines. I thought we were well suited. We'd known each other for a hundred years, spent hours together socially, although not a lot of it alone, but somehow I didn't notice that. Then we married and we were 'alone together,' as they say." She paused. "It seemed that he didn't want to be alone together with me." He watched as her eyes misted over with tears.

"I'm sorry."

"Well, I've gone this far now. Mr. Fleming, when you said just now that he was seeing a psychiatrist, I was glad. I am very sorry that the poor doctor is dead—apart from anything else, perhaps Martin would have continued his therapy. You see, I had suggested once that he go."

"May I ask why?"

She paused, and James could see that she was weighing her words. "Our marriage was never consummated, Mr. Fleming. It was so hard for me. At first I thought it was that I was unattractive. But watching him struggle, trying, you know, and then the humiliation. I assured him that I loved being his wife, that we could live a happy life together without all that, other, well, physical side. But he came to detest the sight of me. I reminded him of his inability, I think, in that regard. And he's so successful at everything he does. I think he just couldn't stand it. Mr. Fleming, if he was going to kill anybody, he would have killed himself. But of course there was no question of that. The divorce was all very civilized and all very quiet. Mrs. Edwards, that's his mother, made sure of that."

"She hadn't wanted him to marry?" James was struck by this bit of information, suddenly reminded of his own mother.

Mrs. Edwards was silent.

"Some mothers are possessive, I suppose," he added.

"It was more than that." Mrs. Edwards sighed as she plucked some dead flowers from their stalks. "Let me show you the rest of the garden, and my view of the sea—my inspiration."

James felt she had confided even more than he could have expected, and he refrained from pressing her for more details. They moved through her kitchen into the long, narrow, walled garden, breathing in the bracing sea air that moved across the water, blue and friendly beneath them—as blue as she had captured in her paintings. As they strolled back to the house, she held out her hand. "I do hope you find the murderer, Mr. Fleming. All I can tell you is that it won't be Martin."

It was dark when James finally drove up to the Darcy house. He could see lights were on, and Mrs. Darcy's car parked behind Darcy's in the driveway. With some trepidation, he rang the bell. Joan Darcy herself opened the door, her face immovable, her expression blank.

"Oh, it's you," she greeted him. "What do you want now?"

"I'd like to talk to you—please," he added.

"Not tonight."

"Just five minutes? And perhaps I won't have to bother you again?"

She looked tired, and James had a pang of guilt, but not quite enough to back off. His belief that she had cuckolded Tom had hardened his heart. As he entered the room he noticed a tall young man leaving for the back of the house, and they both heard the back door shut with a thud.

"Your son?"

"Yes—he's going to a friend's for some company," said Joan, sitting stiffly on the sofa. "Get to the point."

"All right, Mrs. Darcy. Did you ask your husband for a divorce, and did he agree to give it to you?"

Mrs. Darcy looked over her shoulder quickly to see if her son was quite gone, and then turned back angrily to James.

"That is none of your business. Why are you here?"

"Mrs. Darcy, I believe that you and Mr. Watson were having an affair. I believe you wanted out of your marriage. If Dr. Darcy refused that would give you a motive."

"You were right, Mr. Fleming! This is indeed the last time you'll ever see me. If you come near me again I'll call my lawyer. My marriage was virtually nonexistent for two or three years now. Tom had only one love—his patients. I'd put up with that, and yes, I wanted out! But I just buried a man that I once loved. When he was young and passionate. When he had brown curly hair and we went dancing all night. The man I loved and with whom I had a beautiful baby boy." Joan's voice thickened with tears. "I am mourning that man and I am feeling very bad that perhaps I made these last weeks difficult. I was angry with him—yes—but I would never have harmed him—physically. Now get out."

Joan said it very softly but James heard the resolve in her voice, and he left quickly, murmuring apologies.

Very uneasy at what he'd just done, he started his engine, noting a car pulling slowly down the cul-de-sac, its lights already doused. He was glad that Joan Darcy would have some company to offset the emotions his own visit had caused.

When James finally reached home he dropped onto his bed, exhausted from the day. The funeral had been draining enough, and now it seemed it had taken place days ago, not just that morning. He rolled over to see if the light was shining on his answering machine, and his heart fluttered for a moment. It was. Geraldine at last, he thought, pressing the button.

There were two messages.

The first was from Whelan, telling him briefly that it looked like they could eliminate Mary as a suspect, because she'd been admitted to the hospital quite early Friday morning, having tried to slit her wrists. Darcy had admitted her, and the nurses said that her husband had been there with her all of Friday and Friday night. Whelan didn't think he could have killed Darcy and gotten back to the hospital and not have been noticed as absent. Still, James speculated, there was a possibility.

The second message wasn't from Geraldine either. It was from Walsh. A terse statement telling James that when they unlocked Darcy's filing cabinet with the key they had found in his waistcoat pocket, the top drawer had been completely empty. The bottom drawer, which had given the cabinet its weight, had been filled merely with textbooks and medical journals.

James quickly dialed Mrs. Fogarty. She herself was still stunned. Walsh had already phoned her and she had explained that she'd never had a key, that Dr. Darcy did the filing himself. She only handed him the folders when she'd finished typing notes. As far as she knew, there was no other key.

Flummoxed, James lay on his bed thinking, and he found himself there, fully dressed, as the weak morning sun roused him the next day.

CHAPTER
—— 24 ——

DETERMINED TO ELIMINATE some of the suspects on his list, James drove to the address that he had for Mr. Mullins. He assumed that the man would be at work, but perhaps there'd be a wife at home to tell him his place of business. Mrs. Fogarty's memory didn't extend that far!

He parked in front of a very ordinary semidetached house in Ranelagh and walked quickly to the front door. He'd had a strange sense of urgency that morning, a feeling that the murderer most likely was a man. The files would have been numerous and consequently heavy. To his thinking, a woman dragging a bag of any kind would have been remembered. Yet as Walsh had told him, no one had come forward with any information, anything at all.

A short, stout woman with a frowning face opened the door. Her gray hair fell close around her round head like a helmet.

She snapped at him as he asked for Mr. Robert Mullins.

"Why do you want to see him?"

"That's private, I'm afraid."

"Nothing he does is private," she snapped again, glaring at him.

"Are you Mrs. Mullins?"

"Who's asking?"

"My name is James Fleming. I'm a solicitor."

"So what are you soliciting?"

"Look, are you his wife?" James was aggressive now.

"His wife? Hah!" her sharp retort was like a branch breaking. "My own husband is inside. Robert will never get married. Here, come in. See for yourself."

She roared his name and Robert emerged from the back rooms of the narrow house. When James spoke to him he began to tremble.

"Go in the sitting room, you fool," his mother said, pushing him ahead of her. "Bill, Bill," she roared. "Wake up." An older man in his sixties stirred in his chair. He looked up sheepishly and then stood, ignoring everybody.

"Bill," the woman roared yet again. "Get out of here. This man wants to see Robert. God knows why. Apparently, it's a private matter." Her sarcastic voice mimicked James's accent.

She slammed the door and James jumped inadvertently at the sound.

As James explained who he was and why he had come, Robert's trembling increased, but now, James noted, it was accompanied by the most amazing sweat. It formed in beads and ran down his pallid brow and cheeks as he vainly mopped it away.

"Mr. Fleming, I beg of you. Don't mention any of this to my mother. She never knew about Dr. Darcy, and she would kill me if she knew."

James thought he could well believe it, but this man was in his late twenties, at least. Still living at home, still under his mother's thumb. If Mullins murdered anyone it would be that mother!

"But you saw him that day. You might be able to help," James said kindly. "I won't tell your mother about it."

Tears filled Mullins's eyes and James wanted to flee.

"Go on," he said, resisting the urge.

"I told a lie and then Dr. Darcy helped me make it not a lie. I went to the bookies, like he said." Mullins smiled briefly. "I laid a bet," he said carefully, as if practicing new words. "And God, I won, I won three pounds." His face fell and tears flowed. "I told Dr. Darcy at my session. He was very proud."

"Yes, I'm sure. I am pleased for you."

James studied the wreck of a man in front of him. The helmeted woman was now banging on the door with the flat of her hand, and he knew their time was limited. What to do.

"Mr. Mullins, do you work? Do you have a job?" Mullins shook his head. James heard himself talking and wondered at himself: "I need someone at work to do photocopying. It is a little boring. You stand at the copying machine and just copy many, many papers. Perhaps if you could come each afternoon? My office manager, Maggie, would show you what to do and it would be a big help to her. And of course you would be paid." Maggie will skin me now, for sure, he added in his head.

James had seldom seen such astonishment and gratitude in a single expression. The man nodded just as the door flew open.

James leapt up.

"Mrs. Mullins," he said, "our interview went well. Robert starts next Monday." James was proud of his ruse. He handed his card to Robert, and one to his mother. He shook Robert's wet and trembling hand.

"Good day to you," James said overly formally to the woman, and stopped her in her tracks, he thought. He walked purposefully from the room and the house, but he couldn't shake her. The woman grabbed his arm as he attempted to open his car door.

"You don't fool me," she hissed, as she waved his card in his face. "You're a lawyer. You said so, and it's on your card. You've come about the letters, haven't you?"

James tried to keep the amazement out of his face as he suddenly saw in his mind's eye the cheap stationery and the clumsy threats.

"Just tell me why, and I'll see what I can do," he said.

"That fool in there, he thinks I don't know about him creeping off to his psychiatrist. Of course I know. The GP told me and he told me not to interfere with him. But I just wanted that witch doctor to know that he didn't fool everybody."

"Dr. Darcy is dead!" James felt nothing but disgust for this woman as he realized it was she who had composed and sent the ugly letters to Tom.

"I'll deny this if you tell anybody."

"I'll do what I see fit." James leaned into her face. "And I will expect Robert to report for work on Monday." Pushing past her he got in his car, and phoned Walsh, and then Whelan, with this news. One more suspect off the list.

"Not in a thousand years," James said to Whelan over the phone.

"Why, because he cried, because he sweats? Jaysus, Fleming, don't quit your day job."

"Very funny. You know, I do have some sense of people, Whelan. Mullins wouldn't kill the one person who gave him hope and help and some affection."

"Fleming, the mother could be covering for him and the letters."

"No, believe me, I met her."

"So according to you, Mullins is out—apparently because he's henpecked?"

"Yes." James didn't dare tell Whelan he'd hired the man.

"Right." Whelan sighed. "And I think Mary's husband, Brian, is out. The nurses were adamant."

"Elizabeth is still a possibility—she has killed before."

"Emily?"

"No, I spoke with her myself. She had no motive, trust me. I think I'd put Elizabeth ahead of her for now."

"You're going there next?"

"No, today I've got to go to court to file some papers for an actual paying client." James laughed. "If I don't get paid, you'll never get paid. Look, maybe you could visit Walsh—see if he'll give up any of his thoughts about the empty filing cabinet. You know him from the old days, if I'm not mistaken. Ask him about fingerprints? Or the weapon—anything like that." He sighed.

"You know, Fleming, if you think about it, this murderer was a very smart bastard. There is no weapon. The files are missing. No one saw or heard anything unusual. I'll bet you there are no fingerprints—"

James shivered. "When you say it like that, it reminds me of Darcy's horse. No one saw anything. It was quick. No weapon found. He cut the horse's throat . . ." James fell silent.

Whelan was silent too.

"You think it could be the same person?"

"Yes," James said at last. "I do."

As soon as James disconnected from Whelan, the phone rang again and he sighed. It was Maggie.

"James, where are you?"

"Well, I am sitting in my car. I'm beginning to get very cold. The rain is pouring down the windscreen, and I've just hired some kind of emotionally disabled man to come in and do the copying for you."

"Oh," he heard Maggie say in a small voice.

"Well, you asked," he said jovially, picturing Maggie's pretty, lively, challenging face.

"James," she said softly, "we've got to change moods now. I've got some very bad news." James thought instantly of his mother, but Maggie went on quickly.

"It's about Mrs. Darcy . . ."

"Yes?"

"She's dead."

James went blank for some seconds, a darkness rushing through him.

"What did you say? She's dead?"

"Yes, murdered. Her son found her when he came home around midnight last night."

"Oh my God, her son?"

"I know. First the father, then his mother. I'm sorry, James." Maggie's voice was sad and frightened. "What are you going to do?"

James thought for a while.

"Maggie, I really do have to go to court to file papers on the Franklin estate. Then . . . God, I don't know, I'll get back to you." James hung up. He knew he could not face going back to that house. He also knew he hadn't asked Maggie how Joan had died. He didn't want to know, he definitely did not want to know that.

CHAPTER

——— 25 ———

JAMES'S CONSCIENCE PRESSED on him throughout the rest of the day, and it was with a burden of dread that he dragged himself from the Four Courts to Walsh's office and sat heavily in the chair across from the older man.

"This is a first, Fleming," said Walsh.

"I've come about Joan Darcy."

"I see." Walsh was slow to react. "Do you know anything yet?"

"You mean details? No."

"Her throat was cut. But this time there was a struggle."

"Oh, God." James grew ashen and closed his eyes.

"Fleming?" Walsh's voice was sharp and called James back to himself. "What's the matter with you?"

"I saw Mrs. Darcy last night." His voice was leaden.

"What!"

"It was around seven-thirty, eight o'clock. I went to her house—"

"The day of the funeral!"

"I had had an idea. I had pieced together a scenario that Mrs. Darcy and a co-worker, Watson, were having an affair. I had thought that if Darcy had refused to consider a divorce, then that gave one or both of them a motive. I sounded out Watson and I wanted to sound her out too. Yes, I went the night of the funeral, knowing she'd be tired and vulnerable—"

"Jaysus, Fleming."

"I know, I know." James waved his hands in the air. "She got angry, of course. When I arrived, her son left. I don't know if he would have anyway, or if he left because someone, me, had called to the house. He didn't see me, he didn't know me. I don't think he would have left on my account . . ." He looked at Walsh, hoping he would confirm that.

"The boy's in terrible shape, Fleming," was all Walsh said as he shook his head sadly. "Both parents inside of a week. And he's an only child."

"I feel guilty enough already, Walsh," James said.

"Why?"

"Well, I might have been the last person to see her alive. I had upset her when I was there. She was tired and perhaps our hostile exchange had lowered her guard. I upset her and then within hours she is murdered and now, from what you tell me, she confronted her murderer, knew for some split second—or longer—that she was going to die a horrible, violent death!"

The two men were silent a long time.

"Did she say anything to you—any clue as to if she were expecting anybody?"

"No. Wait, that reminds me—I remember feeling relieved she was going to have company."

"Yes?" Walsh sat up straight in his chair.

"When I was pulling away from the house I noticed a car coming up behind me, slowly. You know it's a dead-end street. I assumed someone was coming to condole with her and I was glad."

"For chrissakes, man. The model, the make, the color?"

"That's just it, Walsh. The headlights were already switched off—"

The two men looked at each other at that instant of revelation.

"The killer," was all Walsh said.

James gave his statement to the police as required, and although the process only took an hour, it felt like years to him. Almost feverish, he had an overwhelming desire to go to sleep. Only oblivion could make him stop dwelling on the scene in his imagination: the killer driving up behind him as he drove away, the killer waiting in the car, approaching the house, being admitted, attacking Joan in her own sitting room, slashing at her. Walsh had said there was blood throughout the room.

That pristine room. The home that Darcy had inhabited only a week before—less than a week before. Friday morning he would have left that house to go to work. James pictured him leaving, thinking of his patients and the day ahead, perhaps looking forward to his return that night. Having a drink, a brandy from that trolley which James had seen, tossing aside his suit jacket, perhaps stretching his legs, resting them on the ottoman, glad that it was Friday night, the start of the weekend. But Darcy never came home that Friday night. James counted on his fingers as he sat waiting for the statement to be typed. Saturday, Sunday, Monday, Tuesday—Joan survived him by just four days.

God, he had been so wrong. How had he spun some marital difficulties into a murderous scenario? She had been no Lady Macbeth. But just a woman, fed up, missing what she'd once had, looking for some love or companionship, or to feel young and sexual. Watson was a user, but perhaps she hadn't known that. It had all been a domestic drama, a husband and wife realizing they were no longer in love after a long and stable marriage; the fire was gone, dullness had set in. What had he been thinking? His stomach rolled over. He had better start thinking clearly now.

He drove to the nearest pub, and leaving the car where it would be safe until the morning, he went in and sat down in a corner, folding his long lanky frame into the small dark space. It was a local pub and the patrons looked at him inquiringly. He was an outsider, but since he was quiet and of no real interest, they turned away. He sat and steadily drank his way through six pints of Guinness until the pub closed, and then he had the barman phone for a taxi.

Unsteadily he entered his empty flat and sat on the cold black leather sofa. He had thought vaguely that Geraldine might be there, waiting. She had a key. But she wasn't. At least Darcy had had a wife, even if their marriage had fallen on hard times. They were still husband and wife.

She was the person closest to him. If the killer had wanted to avenge himself or herself on Darcy, as James had also assumed was the motive for the horse's death, surely it made more murderous logic to kill Joan first and thereby cause Darcy great pain and suffering. Why kill Darcy and then Joan?

James made some very strong coffee and stood at the counter in his kitchen, jotting down thoughts as they came. He had a nagging feeling he was not seeing the connection that was there.

The fact the files were missing said plainly now that the murderer had been afraid that something he'd confided to Darcy was in the files. And had also, of course, James added to himself, been retained in Darcy's memory.

Kill Darcy—thereby kill the memory. Kill Darcy—eliminate the written record of the terrible secret. Kill Joan—why? To kill what might be in her memory too.

That was it! The murderer believed that Darcy had confided in his wife. And he killed her after Darcy, perhaps because he had not known Darcy was married until the murder was reported in the papers. The killer had made his move against her only after the funeral, when the police, who had been in and out of her house until then, had finally left her in peace.

Then why did James still have the nagging feeling that he'd been the one to lead the murderer there?

"Christ!" exclaimed James as his head cleared completely. He had led him to Joan, but not in his car that night. He intimated to Edwards that Darcy's wife was a suspect, and his secretary also. The two people closest to Darcy. It was he, James, who had planted the seed.

But in reality, it was Mrs. Fogarty who knew far more than Joan ever did. Darcy didn't discuss his patients with her, but Mrs. Fogarty knew details.

James hands were trembling as he dialed Mrs. Fogarty's number. A sleepy, alarmed voice answered quickly.

"Joe?"

"No, It's James Fleming."

"I thought it was my drunk of a husband," she said, coming awake. "Look at the time. Why are you phoning me in the middle of the night, Mr. Fleming?"

"Anne, listen, you're in danger. I can't go into it now. I'm going to call the police. Don't open the door to anyone, do you hear me! I'll be coming and you'll know it's me. Otherwise don't open the door."

"Oh dear."

James hung up on her frightened voice and dialed Walsh's home number, which he'd managed to extract from him only that day.

The two men drove up simultaneously in front of Mrs. Fogarty's small house. Walsh was on the phone. No one was answering at Edwards's house. He dispatched a police car with instructions to have him watched, and followed if he went out. James ran up to the front door. Lights were being switched on as the neighbors, ever alert, got up "to see" what trouble the husband was causing now.

Anne, now fully dressed, let James and then Walsh in and led them to her kitchen, indicating the sleeping children upstairs.

"Is your husband home?"

"No, he's on a binge. It could be days. What's going on?" Anne said, looking truly frightened. "I heard about Mrs. Darcy on the news."

"That's just it, Anne," said James. "The theory is that the killer went after Joan because Dr. Darcy might have told her a secret this patient doesn't want known. I think then he'll figure out you might also know confidential information— in fact, if I can say this, I am surprised he didn't go after you first."

"That's the thing, Fleming," said Walsh. "There are a thousand Fogartys in the phone book. This killer wouldn't be able to find her that easily. He would have had to have known her husband's first name, or known her car perhaps, and then followed her home. But if all this only dawned on him since Darcy's killing, he wouldn't have had the chance to do that. I think Mrs. Fogarty would have been first but he couldn't find her."

"But it would only be a matter of time." James added. "If it is Edwards, he has money and resources to find something like this out fairly quickly."

"Mr. Edwards?" Mrs. Fogarty was shocked.

"Yes, I'm sorry, Anne, I shouldn't have sprung it on you like that. I think he is our strongest suspect—"

"At least for now," added Walsh firmly.

"But why do you suspect him? And why would he come after me? That man only had trouble sleeping. The only things I typed about him were poor Dr. Darcy's careful notes on his prescriptions for his medications!"

"And that's all you know?" Walsh asked.

"As God is my witness. Look, I know nothing that would be a threat to anybody. Dr. Darcy kept his own handwritten case notes. I typed formal records for him. Those and his notes were in the manila folders in the file. Those folders were thick, some of them, I saw that they were handwritten but I never read them. I wouldn't have, but Dr. Darcy was always very careful."

"Well, Edwards, or someone else, feels threatened by what you might know."

"What's going to happen?"

"I'm going to put men on around the clock, Mrs. Fogarty, to guard you. I'd ask you to stick close to home."

"Can I go shopping?'

"Locally, that's all."

She looked questioningly at Walsh. He smiled. "You're right. I haven't got this all worked out yet, Mrs. Fogarty. My main thought tonight was to see that you were safe."

"If you want to use me as bait I'll do it," she said straightforwardly.

Walsh and James talked this over quietly for a while as Mrs. Fogarty put on the tea. Walsh radioed the car in Foxrock. They reported Edwards's car to be at home.

"I think she is fairly safe for now," said Walsh.

James agreed. "If Edwards had pulled onto this road half the neighborhood would have seen the car."

"I know. But no one on Darcy's cul-de-sac saw a car that night. They didn't see yours and they didn't see Edwards's—we've got the make and model and so on. There are only seven houses on that road and it seems everyone had their curtains drawn, the VCR or the CD players going. They were, one and all, isolated and uninvolved."

"You did the interviews yourself?"

"Yes. I want to get this bastard too you know, Fleming. I didn't know Darcy like you did. But these are two of the most brutal, callous killings I've seen. Whether it turns out to be Edwards or someone else—I'll nail him to the wall."

"Not before I do," added James. "Right, so where do we go from here?"

"If our theory is correct, he'll think he'll have to move against Mrs. Fogarty and soon."

"Can we draw him out somehow?" James speculated. "Can we use Mrs. Fogarty without endangering her? Perhaps she could ring him and say she knew something about him, maybe attempt a little blackmail. Arrange to meet him and we'd be there instead?"

Walsh liked the idea, and together they broached Mrs. Fogarty.

Mrs. Fogarty quickly agreed. "It would give me great satisfaction if I could contribute to putting away the man that killed Dr. Darcy."

Walsh was satisfied that the plan did not put her in real danger. The plainclothes officers were in place, so Walsh and James agreed to come back at ten the next morning.

The next day, locked in Mrs. Fogarty's small sitting room and sustained by a pot of strong tea, James and Walsh prepped her on what was about to take place.

Slightly nervous, she took James's cell phone from him and phoned Martin Edwards at his place of work. Following the simple script Walsh had put down on paper, she identified herself as Darcy's secretary and then paused, adding that she had some of Darcy's handwritten notes about their meetings. They watched her face intently and saw as her expression fell. She had been persuasive, they thought, but Edwards had cut her off.

"He said he had no idea what I was referring to. He was very short and to the point. I am sorry."

"Oh, no, Mrs. Fogarty. You were marvelous. This man is either innocent," Walsh paused, clearly now having serious doubts, "or, he's very devious."

"Well, we know he's very intelligent," James broke in. "Look how he's covered his tracks hitherto. He smelled a rat today, perhaps. Sensed a trap. He could have assessed Mrs. Fogarty's nature by just seeing her in Darcy's office—and realized she wasn't a blackmailing type. And of course he's known from the start that I suspected him." James shook his head. "I didn't handle that well—"

"This is not the time for regrets, Fleming. We've got to get creative here. Mrs. Fogarty is still in danger and we have nothing on this man. We have to consider that it could be Edwards, but also that it could be someone else."

After reassuring Mrs. Fogarty and ascertaining the officers knew the drill, James and Walsh went their separate ways. Walsh to headquarters and James to his car which, he mused, was now more of a home to him than his flat.

CHAPTER
—— 26 ——

As James drove, he racked his brains. He wanted to take action and he wanted to take it now. He thought of his past cases, of how he'd laid traps in some, pieced together clues in others. All had ended in a confrontation. James knew in his heart that Edwards was the one. But just confronting him, saying that to his face, would lead nowhere.

Edwards's former wife, Judith, had been very forthcoming during their meeting. Perhaps there was some way to get to him through her.

James phoned ahead and soon found himself once again in the small house in Dalkey. Today the rain clouds hid the sun and the little room was cheery in a different way, with an open fire burning in the old-fashioned grate. Part of him hated to bring death and betrayal into this peaceful scene; part of him drove him onward.

"Is this about Martin again?" Judith asked softly.

"I'm afraid so."

"I know from the news report that the psychiatrist's wife was murdered also. This situation is truly awful."

"It is, and most of all for their son," James said.

"He's young?"

"Young enough, twenty-three."

"Oh God, that's hard. Since you are here, I take it you are still suspicious of Martin?"

"Yes, and I know you don't believe it is possible that he could kill. So I am going to ask you to help prove that he's innocent."

"I'm really not sure about any of this, Mr. Fleming. You can tell me your thoughts, but I'm not agreeing to take part in any proving..." Her voice was sharper.

"Understood. Just hear me out, please. Darcy is dead. His files were stolen and I think we can assume they are destroyed. But I believe the killer is still in fear that Darcy had shared his secret with other people, namely his wife, who's now dead. And possibly his secretary, who now lives in fear.

"Mrs. Edwards, I personally think that the killer might be your former husband. I believe that because I think I planted the fear of exposure from another source in his mind. For the sake of this argument, my premise is that the killer, your former husband, Edwards, will go after anyone he thinks Darcy confided in. I am proposing that you..." James hesitated. "Well, I am suggesting that you help me prove, or disprove, that by pretending that Dr. Darcy called you in for a consultation, that you know Martin's secret—"

"Mr. Fleming, but I don't know any secret!"

"Don't you?" James held his breath.

"You don't mean? What, that he was impotent? Why would Martin kill because of that? It's ridiculous. I think I said that the last time. If that is the so-called secret, then I was the first to know it."

"I agree. But I don't think it's that. I think it is something more powerful. It has to be—to drive a man to kill like this. The killer is someone protecting something very valuable—his secret. This secret, if it is revealed, would destroy him. This secret is driving him to kill."

"Mr. Fleming." Judith's voice was even stronger now. "I absolutely do not believe Martin killed the doctor or his wife. I have known him for many, many years. However, in order to prove that to you and show some loyalty to my former husband, I will attempt to help you."

Chagrined at her adamancy, James carried on, suppressing his own doubts. Quickly he outlined his plan. "We have to act fast, Ms. Edwards, for him to give any credence to your phone call."

She finally agreed to try to set up a meeting with her husband, that night if possible, and James called Walsh to inform him of what he'd done.

"I don't know, Fleming. At least Mrs. Fogarty was close to the situation—she had some credibility. Even then, Edwards didn't fall for it. You are convinced somehow that he is the killer, but

I'm not. All you've got pointing at him is a bad attitude, as they say. He's angry, and he's nervous. We've got nothing on him."

"But that's the point! We've got to get him to show his hand. Ms. Edwards has agreed, because she's convinced he's innocent."

"He may well be."

"Then we'll know that for certain."

Walsh reluctantly gave in, saying that James could rehearse Ms. Edwards.

"If this is going to happen, you must let me know about it, Fleming," Walsh said crossly.

"Of course. I'll get back to you."

James listened with his heart in his throat as Judith Edwards phoned her ex-husband. She was clearly very nervous and her voice trembled, but James thought this only lent credibility to what she was saying.

He waited as she spoke the key sentence:

"You know, Martin, this business with Dr. Darcy and his wife is very tragic."

She waited as Edwards said something.

"The reason I mention it to you is that . . ." She paused, and James felt the sweat gather on his palms—would she go on?

". . . I know that you were seeing Dr. Darcy . . ." Another pause as she listened to Edwards. James could hear the man's voice grow louder.

"Martin, Martin. You sound so upset. Yes, I know you were seeing him, because he invited me in for a consultation—"

She jumped nervously as Edwards shouted.

"He was very worried about you, he said he wanted to help you. He thought I could perhaps help you also."

She listened. "Yes, I know what he knows, I mean, knew."

Another pause.

"Of course, dear, you can come tonight, around nine." Judith put the phone down thoughtfully and then looked at James.

"He asked me if I knew his secret, Mr. Fleming. And I lied, you made me lie to someone I love."

"To clear his name, Ms. Edwards, his name and yours."

"But you don't believe that at all. If you are right, Mr. Fleming, I will be helping you trap him."

"Ms. Edwards, I have met this man once. I have certain theories. You have known him many years. We are weighing those two things in the balance. You are convinced he's innocent; this will prove it to me. If you are right, by tonight it will be all over and you'll never have to see me again or be troubled by this situation."

She still looked doubtful. "What am I to say to him? I don't know his secret—if he has one. Really, Mr. Fleming, I feel you've rushed me into something."

James saw her wavering and glanced at his watch. "Ms. Edwards, I can work out with you what you would need to say to him. In a way, it's very straightforward, pretty much based on what you've already indicated to Edwards on the phone just now. We have at least a couple of hours. He agreed to the time?"

"Nine? Yes. He said he had things to do . . ."
she paused. "He'd hardly go riding on such a
windy day." She glanced out the small window,
across the road at the shrubs and bushes blowing
in the stiff breeze.

"Sorry? What did you say? He's going riding?"
James was intent.

"I don't know, but, yes, he's a fine horseman.
Keeps a horse in Enniskerry. Or at least he did
when we were married." She sighed. "Why do
you ask?"

"Oh, I ride myself, that's all," he added
offhandedly.

James went on making small talk, but he was
uneasy. She was plainly restless and, he sensed,
having second thoughts.

"I think you are reluctant to do this, Ms.
Edwards, but I can't stress strongly enough that
what happens tonight will be definitive. It will
confirm one way or another Edwards's involvement in these events. You are convinced Edwards
is innocent, and, if nothing else, it will give you a
chance to see him again."

Judith's face lit up. "You know, Mr. Fleming, I
have a feeling this will work out. I've gone this
far—I'll see it through." She stood up with
renewed energy. "Now, I have some work to finish, brushes to wash and some cleaning to do.
And some food to prepare. I'm not going to let
Martin come all this way and not have a nice
supper ready for him when he gets here."

James, aware he'd outstayed his welcome for
the moment, suggested he drive on into the vil-

lage for an evening meal. This way he could phone Walsh and arrange the setup, and walk back, leaving his car out of sight. But he didn't tell her all that.

"I'll be back here at seven, Ms. Edwards. Mr. Walsh will also arrive then. That will give us plenty of time, two hours, to go over what you need to say. When Edwards arrives, we'll remain in the kitchen while you talk with him. If all goes well, as you expect, then we'll stay in there and Edwards will never know about it. Your mind and ours will be clear on his innocence." He paused briefly. "If, on the other hand—"

"What? When he goes to kill me, you will rush to my rescue? How very dramatic." James was amazed to see her smile at him.

"Ms. Edwards, if he threatens to harm you, yes, we will intervene."

CHAPTER
27

H AVING PARKED HIS car on the outskirts of the village, James wandered down the main street on foot and finally sat in one of the small trendy restaurants . . . eight tables crowded into space for four. The bright shiny wood, the butcher-block style of decor, was not to his personal taste, but he wanted a place that was quiet so that he could order his thoughts. Hungry as always, he willingly studied the small handwritten menu painstakingly decorated with delicate watercolor illustrations of herbs. Dismayed at the choices, he at last placed an order with the extremely bored but rather bohemian-looking young woman who seemed also to be the chef. The wild night had kept diners away, she explained, as she reappeared with his selection.

The bread he'd ordered, made with eighteen different grains, tasted like glue. He didn't even know there were eighteen grains, he mused dejectedly. The cheese selection was good; after all, how could they ruin cheese? The salad of walnuts and celery and some odd fennel-like thing was disastrous, and James left it to one side and drew out his notebook and pen. The coffee and enormous slice of Belgian chocolate cake cleared his mind as he settled to focus on what Judith could say to Edwards when he came.

Edwards. From the beginning, James hadn't liked the man, but now doubts assailed him. He wondered at his own impetuosity. Enticing the man to Dalkey, manipulating Judith into playing a role in this melodrama . . . he wondered at himself. Why, after all, had he locked onto Edwards more than any other of Darcy's clients?

He sipped his coffee. Clearly, at the beginning, Edwards was just one of many who could have been suspects; still were, in fact. Mrs. Fogarty had played her part in helping to eliminate some, yet they would all have to be checked out too, if this enterprise with Edwards failed tonight.

What of the others? James jotted down their names. Mr. Mullins? He had assessed him as not capable of hurting Darcy because of his affection for him. Emily? James really didn't think so, but he also had to admit he had personal reasons for eliminating her from the list. Mary and her husband, Brian—now definitely out, because of the time frame. Elizabeth and her husband Ciaran— no motive he could think of.

James sighed more loudly than he thought. The bohemian chef was at his side in a flash, refilling his cup. He smiled at her and she smiled

back. For a moment he was removed from the
entirety of his situation: Edwards and Judith,
Ger and Sarah, Darcy, death. For a moment,
there seemed infinite possibilities in the young
woman's deep blue eyes, the full black brows, the
west of Ireland white skin. He liked her smile
and the way she moved in her loose-fitting dress.
He thought he smelled heather and felt clean
wind blowing across his face. But it was the wind
from the open door, and as he watched, bereft,
she turned away to gratefully greet another
patron. James shook himself.

No, he hadn't liked Edwards. He knew that
much. He hadn't liked the man, he admitted to
himself, because he didn't like in him what he
saw in himself. The stiffness, the propriety of the
Protestant middle class. He also hadn't liked the
brittleness of the exterior man. Or the arrogance.
And he hadn't liked the fine house, the success in
business, the accomplished mother. What was
wrong with all of that? he asked himself honestly.
Nothing to speak of, he answered. But what he
hadn't liked was the extreme coldness of the
man. Hard and cold.

But James did like Judith. Edwards was a fool
to have left her, he thought. That said a lot about
the man.

James felt reassured. It wasn't so much his
own dislike of Edwards but his reading of the
man's anger at Darcy when he'd heard it on the
tape. Yes, that had been his first clue. And then
at his only meeting with Edwards, there had
been the anger and the anxious demeanor of the

man himself. His insistent concern about confidentiality, about the files. Yes, James knew that his instincts were right; he knew he had picked up on Edwards' sense of betrayal, his negative attitude toward Darcy. There was no doubt Edwards had a secret. James reviewed the connections. The killer had a secret, communicated it to Darcy, and then feared Darcy had told Joan. James decided his thinking on this had been clear also: first Darcy, then Joan. Now, Judith's "claim" to know the secret was the way to flush Edwards out. James felt a renewed conviction, a rush of adrenaline.

Again he reviewed the physical evidence. The letters, the scratches on the car, the horse's death, Darcy's death. The letters wouldn't have been Edwards's style at all, and Mullins's mother had cleared that up. The police had ruled out the scratches as in fact random and meaningless. So that was cleared up too. Those too wouldn't have been Edwards's style. The horse. Well, James thought smugly, he knew now that Edwards rode, and in Enniskerry, and at the same stable. The weapon? Common and available. A knife each time. The killer getting bolder each time.

God, he shivered at the memory of Darcy's body and Joan's murder. What was he thinking? If he were right tonight, and not merely trying to prove a hunch, he'd left Judith in real jeopardy. Better to run through what she would say to Edwards with her than sit here speculating about it now. There was no reason that Edwards wouldn't come early. James tossed a twenty-pound note on the table and hurried out of the restaurant.

He shivered. The night had turned wintry, with warm autumnal winds changing to biting icy shafts that sliced through his overcoat. Suddenly the climb up the steep and winding road seemed longer than he'd estimated. He was glad to see, as he reached Judith's house, no car parked outside or on the narrow verge across from it.

A sudden movement inside the window made him pause before he rang the bell. The curtains were drawn, but a sliver of light remained between them, and something, someone, was passing quickly back and forth. He applied his eye to the wet glass and saw a figure, and then the male clothing, and his heart stood still.

Carefully, he drew back from the house. He looked up and down, not a soul, not a car. He cursed as he realized he'd left his cell phone, and everything else, in the boot of his own car. And he cursed again that he had no weapon of any kind and that Walsh wasn't due for another hour.

The houses that abutted Ms. Edwards's were gated and shuttered. Summer homes. The other houses he'd passed on his walk were too far down the road. Why hadn't he noticed how isolated they were? The rain was now driving sleet.

James looked to see how he could get onto the roof. Running to the next house, he threw off his coat and climbed onto the wide window ledge. Fingers wet and now freezing and clumsy, he still managed to grip the overhanging gutter. A chunk of its red clay structure came away in his right hand. The wind was howling now, blowing right off the water, and salt stung his cheeks and eyes. The gutter would not support his weight. He scrambled over. Grasping the drainpipe, testing his weight on the brace that held it to the front wall, he levered himself onto the steep roof. Slowly, slipping on the wet slick surface of the tiles, clinging desperately with fingertips and even his fingernails, he inched upward to the apex and only in the nick of time prevented himself sliding down the far side. Because the houses were built on the granite rock of what was a small mountain, he had no idea how far the drop would be into the garden behind this house. In the pitch black with the wind-driven rain stinging his face, he lowered himself, aimlessly grabbing for any potential handhold and failing utterly to find any. For the last twenty feet or so he slid awkwardly down the roof, hurtled past the gutters at the rear, and collapsed heavily onto the hard ground beneath. Winded but desperate, he scrambled over the dividing garden hedge, heedless of the lancing branches that splintered in his face. The hedge was his springboard to the high cinder-block wall behind it and from the wall he jumped down into Ms. Edwards's garden and ran to the back door, thanking God in His heaven that the knob turned in his hand.

He entered the tiny back hall that he remembered from his earlier visit, and stopping to quiet his heavy breathing, he strained to hear the words from the front of the house. But no words came. The wind screeched off the water still.

Realizing it would also muffle his movements, he moved swiftly and yet stealthily into the kitchen, pacing himself as he planned to advance toward the sitting room.

With a rush of blood to the head, he realized that the sitting room door had been pulled open—the voices could now be easily heard, loud and clear.

"Martin. Martin! I've told you what I know."

It was him.

"Martin, where are you going?"

James, expecting Edwards to be leaving, was struck to stone as he rushed into the kitchen, passing quite near him. The man fumbled wildly for the light switch as Judith followed.

"Stay back!" James shouted. Too late.

Judith had turned on the light, flipping the switch high up at the doorframe.

A yellow hue flooded the brightly painted kitchen, throwing the three occupants into a momentary tableau.

Edwards stared wildly from Judith to James and back.

"You bitch!" he hurled the words at her as realization dawned. "A setup!"

"I'm sorry, Martin. I wanted to prove to him that you had nothing to do with anything. I know you didn't."

James watched as Edwards backed up and glanced quickly at the kitchen drawers, yanked open one and then another, until he found what he wanted. He pulled the carving knife from its sheath. He turned to face them both.

"Stay back!" James screamed again at Judith, but she did not heed him.

Edwards too ignored him. "What exactly did Darcy tell you?" he raged, brandishing the knife at his former wife.

"Nothing. That's the point. I never saw him. Mr. Fleming here put me up to this. I lied ..." Judith Edwards was gasping for breath, shouting too.

"I don't believe you. Fleming here might have set up this trap. But I know you! You wouldn't have gone along with it—not unless you knew something. Now what, what do you know?"

"Put the knife down, Edwards," James said as calmly as he could.

"Why?"

"Because it's over. You betrayed yourself, just coming out here, just picking up that knife."

"I grabbed that for my own protection. A man standing in the dark in her kitchen. Why wouldn't I protect her, and myself? In fact, that's what I'll tell the police—"

"They won't believe you."

"An intruder in the house—I did what I could to save her and myself."

Edwards advanced toward James, who was cornered, his back against the wall. James knew he would have to fight the man. It would indeed look like a struggle. Edwards had nothing to lose.

"Look, Edwards, as of now we have nothing on you. Another step and you put yourself into prison. You know I don't know anything. Your secret, whatever it is, is still safe."

He watched as this registered quickly with Edwards.

"She knows," he said, pointing to Judith with the knife.

"But Martin, I don't know anything. He's right. Please, I love you."

Edwards's face turned toward hers. "I believe you do," he said, his voice suddenly normal. Judith Edwards moved forward instantly, her arms open to embrace him.

In a flash, Edwards reached for her, grasping her hair in his left hand, bringing the knife to her throat with his right.

"Jesus!" James roared.

"Back off, Fleming."

James stood aside helplessly as the two of them moved down the hall toward the front door; Judith, her face frozen in fear and shock, her eyes wide and staring. Edwards held her long hair firmly in his grip as he told her to open the door. They backed out the door—the knife ever at her throat—into the black night.

"Fleming. If you come near us I'll slit her throat—like the others." He moved out of the light that fell from the front doorway. James followed. He could see only darker figures against the dark night. He guessed that that was all Edwards could see of him.

"You won't get away with this . . ." yelled James, wanting to keep Edwards within hearing distance.

"Forget it, Fleming." Edwards's voice was already farther away than James had surmised. He began to run toward it.

"Edwards? Edwards! Judith!" he screamed into the wind, but there was no reply.

James almost passed out as a heavy hand fell on his shoulder.

"Fleming?"

"Walsh? Christ, he's got her. He's taken her out there."

"On foot?"

"So far!"

Walsh radioed his driver and the car swung onto the narrow road a hundred yards behind them and screeched to their side.

"High beams!" screamed Walsh as they moved slowly down the lane.

Nothing.

"They could be anywhere!" yelled James.

"Radio for help, and put out the make and number on Edwards's car," Walsh ordered the driver.

Walsh reached in to the passenger seat, grabbed two large torches, and tossed one to James. The two men switched them on and ran down the road on either side, flashing them side to side, forward and back. Now they were at the seafront. The narrow steep drop to the rocks and strand below revealed itself in the probing shafts of their flashlights.

The rain was still falling heavily but the wind had abated sufficiently for them to call out Edwards's name.

Nothing.

Then one high faint screaming sound. It might have been a gull if it had not been night. It might have been a night bird if it hadn't been for the rain.

"Oh God," yelled James as he and Walsh scrambled down the cliff, slipping and grabbing on to small scrub and wind-beaten branches, grasping on to thorns and thistles.

Flashing their lights wildly in every direction, they spotted beneath them on the sand a patch of white. Heading toward it pell-mell, they fell to their knees beside the still form, drenched and disheveled. The blood from her neck was mingling with the rain and the seawater that was running in on a full tide, dragging at her hair, rushing in over her stricken face and her wide-open eyes.

James knelt in the water and lifted Judith to a sitting position, pushing her hair and the weeds out of her face.

"Over here, please! Oh Judith, what have I done? I never thought it would come to this. Please! Live, Judith, live! Oh God, I am so sorry!" James's voice was increasing in hysteria as the policeman moved him to one side. James was swallowed up in darkness, both real and spiritual. He watched, heart pounding, as the strange silhouette of the policeman bent and unbent, finally straightening to his full height and shaking his head. Tears streamed down James's face and mingled with the rain.

CHAPTER
—— 28 ——

TOGETHER, IN SILENCE, James and Walsh struggled to carry Judith's body to higher ground. They looked up as more uniformed officers with flashlights appeared, beams wavering, searching, in the rain.

"Come here," Walsh hollered. The men arrived, taking the heavy burden from Walsh and James, who stood for a moment to draw breath.

Other lights continued to move toward them.

"Sir, sir?" called a voice. "There's another body down this way."

Walsh and James looked at each other in disbelief.

As they approached the inert body, Edwards groaned. James was filled with a raging desire to kill the man then and there. Two bodies—but naive, gentle Judith was dead; this hideous killer was still alive. James lunged toward Edwards but the police officer grabbed his arm.

"No, Fleming!" Walsh spoke directly into his face. "No."

Edwards lay semiconscious, his leg folded under him in an unnatural position, the broken bone of the compound fracture protruding through the sodden fabric of his trousered thigh. There was nothing to be done, no other way to negotiate the steep side of the cliff, so the officers rigged up a stretcher and carried him laboriously back to the road.

James and Walsh scrambled behind them, Walsh lending a hand when necessary but James refusing to. Muddy, wet, and chilled to the bone, they reached Ms. Edwards's neat and once cozy home. James looked at Walsh with an unspoken query.

"Look, Fleming, I've called for the ambulance but it will take some time to get here obviously. And I want to talk to him if I can, before he goes to the hospital."

Edwards was reviving with the heat of the room and, although obviously in terrible pain, was lucid. He asked for a brandy and James found a bottle in the corner cupboard and poured out a tumbler for each of the three of them.

"I won't talk to you—"

"Walsh is the name," said Walsh in an ominous voice.

"Walsh, I won't talk to you. And I have the right to a solicitor." He grimaced as he moved. "And we have one right here, don't we?" Edwards's eyes glittered as he stared at James.

"I want you to represent me, and then, of

course, whatever I tell you will be confidential. Won't it, Fleming?"

Walsh stood up in disgust. "This is madness," he said, pacing the small room.

"Oh, by no means. I have the right not to talk to you, Walsh, and you know it," said Edwards. "What do you say, Fleming?"

James stared. He despised the man in front of him, loathed him, would perhaps have willingly killed him a mere twenty minutes beforehand. And yet, here he was, here they were, the two of them. Mortal enemies. And despite all that had led to this confrontation, despite or perhaps because of the evil perpetrated upon innocent people, James wanted to hear what this man had to say. He had seen him in action with Judith; he had seen his handiwork—Tom's life-less body, his sad and empty face. Twice now James had personally witnessed the results of this man's evil, and his curiosity was overwhelming. He had to know, he always had to know, the secret, the reason, the motive. He weakened. James's obsession to see into the heart of evil and understand it overtook his better judgment—as always.

"I'll represent you to the degree I will brief your barrister," he said stiffly.

"Fine," said Edwards, glancing at Walsh.

"And I won't accept more than one pound in fees."

"How scrupulous of you."

"Look, Edwards, I knew Darcy—I liked Judith—don't push me too far!"

Edwards shrugged. "I'll talk when Walsh leaves the room."

Walsh, scowling at James in disappointment, stomped off.

"Talk," said James, pulling his chair nearer to Edwards. He could see his sodden clothes starting to steam in the heat of the fireplace.

Edwards shifted slightly. He was leaning his back against the arm of the sofa, his legs stretched in front of him down the length of it, bound together loosely with now bloodied bandages. The flow of blood had been stemmed, but the pain was asserting itself. He took a large gulp of the brandy.

"The first mistake I made was to confide in Darcy," he began slowly. "It was a secret that was not mine to confide or to share. The day that it happened, that afternoon after my appointment with Darcy, when I truly realized what I had done, what a terrible transgression it was, I was at the stables. I'd gone there to ride, to calm myself. I was well aware that Darcy kept a horse there, even though he was so very careful to keep his private and professional life separate. But I know Killian well—she'd mentioned Darcy in passing. The horse was there—"

"And the knife?"

"Oh, from the kitchen. I'd gone in to get a glass of water. Remember, Fleming, I knew Killian for years . . . I'd often have a cup of tea with her in the kitchen. I saw the knife. It gave me the idea. It was as simple as that.

"When I killed the horse I was wearing my riding jacket. What blood there was when I opened her neck flew onto that. I simply took it off, wrapped the knife in it, and strolled away to my car."

"Incredible," murmured James.

"I felt somehow . . . relieved. The terrible pressure seemed eased. It was like having a boil lanced. Then when I saw Darcy at the next session, I attempted to retract what I'd said to him. But he foolishly wouldn't let go of it. That Thursday when I saw him, I knew it would be my last session. I'd gone home in a rage, like before. Only this time there was no horse, no outlet, no relief. I was very distraught but I took a number of sleeping pills and managed to get through the night. And through the week. I might have continued in that fashion except for the fact that Darcy left a message on my office phone when I didn't show up for my session. On Friday I called Darcy—that's the message that you heard on the tape. I might have left it at that perhaps, if my mother hadn't intervened." He shrugged.

"Your mother?"

Edwards threw him a sharp glance.

"She knew I'd seen a doctor because she'd found my sleeping pills. She stays with me quite often and observed them in my medicine chest— anyway, she knew about my trouble sleeping. That same Thursday afternoon, when Darcy didn't reach me at work, he phoned me at home. Since she was staying with me that week she had answered, and then and there arranged to meet with him. He agreed to see her late on Friday.

"She was quite proud of herself. I think she felt a bit guilty too because she phoned me just before setting out. She was going to discuss my health with Darcy! However, it was easy to convince her that I should meet her at Darcy's office. Ha! The irony was that Darcy had thought it was a great breakthrough—he thought perhaps she had come for therapy! Of course the minute he saw that I had accompanied her, he attempted to get the three of us engaged in a dialogue! He was so lacking in insight, he couldn't understand that she had set up the appointment for the sole purpose of reprimanding him for upsetting me—an old habit since my childhood. I cut the so-called session short. My mother left in her car and I in mine."

James looked at the man, amazed at his equanimity. Apart from grimacing in pain, he was chatting as though all of his story was normal. No remorse. No emotion as he recounted the beginning of a chain reaction that had led to Darcy's death, and that of Mrs. Darcy, and finally his own wife.

"I had realized that Darcy would never let this go. He now had had contact with my mother. There was no knowing if he would confront her with what I had told him. I couldn't take that risk. So, I returned within the hour, alone, to his office, prepared to remedy the situation. I bought the knife at the local shop, near the bookies."

"But the secret, the secret?" whispered James, taut to the point of snapping. He watched as the brandy and the pain and the exhaustion began finally to affect Edwards. The muscles of his face were slackening. The fine patrician features were sagging grotesquely—deep caverns beneath the eyes, gaunt hollows in the cheeks. Even as he spoke his chest seemed to cave in and his hand reached for his leg, gripping it above the fractured bone.

"Yes, you see," he said at last, "I told him we had slept together."

James restrained himself.

"He snatched at that as the cause of all my so-called problems. He, at my last session, had told me she had seduced me, that it was not my fault. That it was hers. That I was an abused child. Ahh, I was hardly a child at fifteen—"

"Pardon?" James blurted.

"You see! *I* knew better. Regardless of what Darcy said or thought, I knew the truth. It is mutual, the attraction. Always was. She is a very attractive woman . . . long flowing black hair, a sensuous figure, a loving mouth . . . If she had ever found out, ever realized that I had betrayed her to Darcy or anybody else, she would never have forgiven me. She would have destroyed me. She has means—financial means, emotional means." Edwards's voice was drifting in and out now. "And we're so happy, have been ever since that foolish interruption of a marriage. Oh, God!" His voice rose in pain.

Edwards's head fell back on the pillows and he groaned mightily. James could hear the arrival of the ambulance and the struggle the men were having to get the stretcher through the narrow front door.

He leapt to his feet, urgency in every part of his being. "Edwards, tell me, did you kill Darcy and Mrs. Darcy . . ." James was panting. "Did you kill him and then Joan Darcy because he might have told your secret? Say it out, say it!"

"Yes."

"And you would have gone after Mrs. Fogarty?"

"The secretary, yes, when I got her alone."

"And tonight?"

"I fully believed Judith knew the secret, fully believed Darcy had phoned her. It made perfect sense to me. You couldn't have known that of course, but nonetheless it was quite clever on your part. Darcy had spoken to Mother. He could easily have pursued Judith. He could have told Judith what he knew and she could have told my mother. Mother would learn of my terrible betrayal of our precious secret."

He closed his eyes and averted his head. "But I see from your face that I was wrong. Judith did not know."

James said nothing.

Edwards looked at him again. "So there was no reason to kill her," he said viciously.

"No." James felt his own guilt and a rising fury strangling him.

He paused, drawing in his breath. "Where are the files?"

"Ashes, every one of them."

The ambulance men were in the room now, pushing James to one side. James moved to let them do their work.

"Edwards? What now?" he asked over their heads.

"When I am charged I'll plead guilty. That way I won't have to reveal any reason, any motive."

James watched in horror as a strange smile spread over Edwards's face.

He waved the men away as he urgently knelt down beside Edwards on the stretcher.

"Why?" he whispered to the injured man. "Why, in God's name, have you told me this horror story? Why me? You aren't even going to use any of this in your defense."

"Exactly. You are right, Fleming. And now *you* can't tell anyone. No more than Darcy did, apparently. He was a man of honor after all."

"But why me—why do you want me to know your rotten corrupt secret?"

"Because living with it will torture you. You will want to tell people. In the oddest places, the strangest times. You will have an urge to tell. It will come to your lips; you will want to speak. And you won't be able to. Remember, Fleming, I know what it is like to live with a secret. I let it slip, once, only once, and see what that has wrought. This situation now is of your own making. If it hadn't been for you, I might never have thought of Darcy's wife. And if you hadn't involved Judith, she'd be sitting right in this room, right now, by her own fire. Instead of me—instead of you."

As the men left with Edwards, Walsh came in, glaring at James, who was standing staring into the fire, watching the flames flare and die, the coals subsiding to embers.

"You can't tell me, can you?"

"No ..." James answered, "No ... But he says ..." James put his hand to his mouth, realizing how close he'd come to blurting something out. He shook his head in sudden despair.

Walsh stared at him.

"Come to the station, Fleming, and make your statement about the events of this evening. But not to me. I'd rather not see your face again tonight." Walsh spat out the words, and they hit.

CHAPTER

29

JAMES WAS EXHAUSTED when he finished at the police station. It was early morning, and tired though he was, he contacted a barrister and briefed him on Edwards's case. The man was pleased to accept on condition of an enormous fee. James agreed, knowing that Edwards or his mother would pay. He no longer cared—the night's events had taken on the quality of a fading nightmare. He felt removed from himself.

He threw himself across his bed. His telephone answering machine was blinking. He sat weary and depressed as he listened to the messages. Geraldine had phoned at last. Did she seem anxious to see him? he wondered idly. He couldn't tell. He didn't care now. He waited. A message from his mother. One from Maggie. Two from Whelan. Yes, he'd get back to them, he said aloud.

The last message, ironically, he thought, as he picked at the threads on his duvet, was from

Sarah. Her cool voice was announcing her return to Dublin on Friday, was instructing him to meet her at the airport, was giving him the arrival time and flight number of her plane. She hadn't asked him to confirm.

Friday, a week to the day that Darcy had died. Friday, when he might have been sitting in Darcy's peaceful office discussing Sarah and Geraldine and his difficulties in making either relationship work. Or whether he would. Or should.

It all seemed so far away now—not petty, not without meaning. Just on the other side of the moon.

James sat up on the side of the bed and held the receiver in his hand, staring at it for a long time. Finally, dialing his travel agent, he asked him to put him on the first flight out to Australia. Geraldine. Sarah. Mother. Work. They'd have to manage without him. Two of them for a very long time indeed.

And maybe, just maybe, on his return, Professor Emily Lawlor would like to take a long walk with him on the pier at Dun Laoghaire, and discuss her thoughts on Coleridge's prose writings, or his thoughts about property law, or the possibility, the hint of a possibility, of a fine future together.